The Changeling

D0055094

Temple City 628

THE WORMLING
BOOK III

The Changeling

JERRY B. JENKINS
CHRIS FABRY

Tyndale House Publishers, Inc., Carol Stream, Illinois

Visit Tyndale's exciting Web site for kids at cool2read.com

Also see the Web site for adults at tyndale.com

TYNDALE and Tyndale's quill logo are registered trademarks of Tyndale House Publishers, Inc.

The Wormling III: The Changeling

Designed by Ron Kaufmann

Edited by Lorie Popp

Published in association with the literary agency of Alive Communications, Inc., 7680 Goddard Street, Suite 200, Colorado Springs, CO 80920.

Library of Congress Cataloging-in-Publication Data

Jenkins, Jerry B.
    The Wormling III : the Changeling / Jerry B. Jenkins ; Chris Fabry.
        p. cm.
    Summary: The Wormling, Owen Reeder, in his continued search for the Son, seeks advice from the Scribe, but along the way is constantly plagued by the Changeling, who can change shapes instantaneously, and is sent by the evil Dragon.
    ISBN-13: 978-1-4143-0157-0 (softcover)
    ISBN-10: 1-4143-0157-X (softcover)
    [1. Good and evil—Fiction. 2. Conduct of life—Fiction. 3. Dragons—Fiction. 4. Adventure and adventurers—Fiction.] I. Fabry, Chris, date. II. Title. III. Title: Wormling three. IV. Title: Changeling.
    PZ7.J4138Wot 2007
    [Fic]—dc22   2006103300

Printed in the United States of America

13 12 11 10 09 08 07
  7   6   5   4   3   2   1

For Jamie

"The world is a dangerous place to live; not because of the people who are evil, but because of the people who don't do anything about it."

ALBERT EINSTEIN

✦

"An utterly fearless man is a far more dangerous comrade than a coward."

HERMAN MELVILLE, *Moby Dick*

✦

"Life is either a daring adventure or nothing."

HELEN KELLER

1

Lair Conversation

Imagine—if you dare—the most hideous, spine-tingling music—screeching violins and long, ominous bass notes that shake the ground. A cacophony of horror is perfect for the scene we are about to describe. For in the darkness of a pungent room, though high and far from what we call earth, sits a being so revolting and gruesome that some have wished we would leave him out of our story. They urge us to shy away from scenes like this, but what would a story be without a villain? How could we measure the good of one character unless we compared it to the bad of another?

Without the being before us, we

would not understand the meaning of *putrid, malevolent, wicked,* or even *appalling.* No, here lies the very heart of our tale, for it is our hero's duty to defeat this foe, to utterly cleanse the world (both the visible and the invisible) of this powerful beast.

At the moment, all we can see is his scaly back, along with his twitching tail. His head bobs at something. Is he eating the flesh of an enemy? Might he be devouring our hero even now? Or picking meat from the bones of some trusted friend of our hero? Or more awful still, could he be torturing someone, trying to pry the whereabouts of our hero from him or her?

As we move into the lantern light in the corner, we clearly see the Dragon's pointed ears encrusted with wax, his long snout with nostrils dripping a gelatinous green substance. The Dragon sniffs it back, and the tongue darts in and out. The moving lips reveal stained, jagged teeth that could snap you in two. Reptilian eyes with dark slits in the centers glow with what seems like fascination or anticipation. And the massive jaw is working.

The body exudes evil power, and it is all we can do to stay in his presence—but stay we must. For he is not chewing or singing or talking to himself or doing anything superfluous. No, he is reading. But these are not words he can truly comprehend, as they are written for someone with a heart, with compassion.

The Dragon shudders and mutters, "The Son, the Son, the Son. That's all you write about, isn't it?" He clears his throat, and a squeak of fire escapes but does not damage the book.

"'The Son shall have power and dominion'?" he chortles. "No. Your prophecies will *not* come true, for your Son is gone, a coward cowering in some corner. He will never be all you want him to be."

The Dragon snarls at a knock behind him and flips another page with a sharpened talon, trying in vain to tear a hole in the book. "What is it?"

Enter RHM, Reginald Handler Mephistopheles (or right-hand man, if you prefer), who would usurp this stinky throne if he could. The two converse in hushed tones, the gist of the vile talk and innuendo concerning our hero and that "We had him right where we wanted him!"

RHM bows his head. "Somehow he defeated your demon vipers and eluded you. But we still have the book—"

"He is getting stronger," the Dragon roars, caring nothing for letting his underling finish a sentence. "Each time he eludes us he becomes more confident."

"Not so strong that he could defeat you, sire."

"Of course not. But if he comes to *believe* he can defeat me, he can harm our plan, all we've worked so hard to accomplish, all we mean to destroy." The Dragon turns back to the book. "These words speak of a new day, countering the rise of *my* kingdom. They suggest a model of the world under the Son's rule."

"Such words would instill a false hope in the people," RHM says. "That is why you have so wisely kept words from them."

"The fact is, *he* found this. The Wormling read it, and the words became part of him. He read far enough to breach the portal; we know that. It's to our advantage that the Son has no idea who he is."

"He can't be far from the castle," RHM says. He draws a circle on an aged map on the wall. "We think he is somewhere within this area, but this Watcher of his alerts him to our flyers, and the tracking device—"

"Has been destroyed. I know." The Dragon flips to the back of the book, brow furrowed as if struggling to grasp the meaning. "It says here—" he taps the page—"that their world will be cleansed by fire."

"Your plan all along, sire."

"Yes," he purrs. "Truly perfect. They will welcome this cleansing as for their own good, and we will strike them down." He turns a furtive eye toward his underling. "It also says that these beings are vulnerable to temptation."

RHM chuckles. "Right you are, sire."

The Dragon growls, and something flashes in his eyes. "Bring the Changeling. I have an important mission for him."

2

Nicodemus

N ow imagine music that changes suddenly, like darkness giving way to sunrise. Beautiful strings announce the light, and French horns welcome the new day.

Nicodemus, a guardian of the light, sits among the tall pines—not that he has to rest or sleep or do anything humans must do, but he chooses to relax and enjoy the pine scent wafting along the hillside and the babble of a stream filled with brown trout. What a stark contrast to the Dragon is this good being, chosen to shadow our hero and guard him.

From the time Nicodemus was first assigned to Owen Reeder (he did not know the boy would turn out to be the Wormling), the tall being has kept the boy in view, seen him discover his identity and grow in strength and knowledge. With each new challenge, Nicodemus has sensed a growing confidence in the lad.

Other invisibles stalking Owen have called Nicodemus out, challenging him as they have the boy. Ever wise and obedient, Nicodemus has held back. Not that it was easy to listen to the taunts of the sniveling invisibles. But Nicodemus has a higher calling.

"Still following the loser?" one would taunt.

"The Dragon will fry him for breakfast," another said. "And you with him."

They made fun of Owen's name, his friends, and even that he carried the magical worm that could breach the portals.

Because these beings knew Nicodemus was following Owen and were themselves seeking the life of his charge, Nicodemus stayed far enough away to throw them off. He withstood the taunts, believing with every ounce of strength in his being that his King would one day win the battle.

When something moved in the treetops, Nicodemus sat up. A streak of light crossed the sky and landed near him. It was Rushalla, one of the King's most trusted messengers.

"What brings you?" Nicodemus said.

The normally pleasant Rushalla gave a grim smile and handed him a parchment. "A message from the King."

"Directly from the Sovereign?"

Rushalla looked away.

Nicodemus scanned the message. "There is no question that this is the King's own hand. But how—?"

"You have sworn to uphold the King's wishes," Rushalla said.

"Did I say I wouldn't?" Nicodemus snapped.

"You look troubled."

"Wouldn't you be? After spending all this time and energy, after literally saving the Wormling's life, I am to pull my protection? pull my watch care?"

"You're implying that *you* are directing his steps?" Rushalla said. "You are the one who has guided him this far?"

"I-I am merely a helper sent by the Sovereign. I have no power beyond that which he gives."

"Or that which he takes away," Rushalla said.

"But what if the Dragon discovers the Wormling's whereabouts? Or if his minions threaten the Wormling's life? Even now a force is massing on the plain."

"Do you suddenly mistrust the Sovereign?"

"Of course not. But in watching this young man, I have picked up some of his ways. I see how he walks through the possibilities of what *might* happen and what *could* happen before he makes a decision."

"You do not think the Sovereign has your charge's best interests at heart?"

"I fear what might happen to him without me."

"The lad has the Watcher. And he has his good heart."

"And he has the entire invisible kingdom arrayed against him," Nicodemus spat. "You know what happened when the Dragon *himself* came after him."

"You think the Sovereign doesn't care?"

Nicodemus hung his head and shuddered. When he could speak, he said, "I'm not worthy. I've disgraced my Sovereign."

"Doubting is not cause for dismissal," Rushalla said. "The Sovereign knows you care. These are only his wishes."

"But to leave the Wormling . . ." He looked at his orders again. "And to watch *this* man . . . by all accounts his situation is hopeless. He is without a Wormling mind. Without much of a mind at all. I am to go there and just wait and hope . . . ?"

"You cannot predict what the Sovereign will do. No one knows his ways or his plans. We simply carry out his wishes."

"I know," Nicodemus muttered. "But this?"

3
Lair Liar

The Changeling was the only being ever to actually saunter into the Dragon's lair. Most cowered, and some even fainted at the possibility of being consumed by the Dragon.

"You know, my brother does some decorating on the side," the Changeling said, picking up a thigh-bone from the floor. "He could spruce this place up. Maybe a couch over here . . ."

A rattle formed in the Dragon's throat.

"A coat of paint can do wonders, you know?" the Changeling said, suddenly wearing an actual coat dripping with paint. "Or perhaps you'd be more impressed with a coat of arms?"

But instead of a knight's outfit, the Changeling turned and pulled on a coat with several sleeves sticking out the front and back, all filled with actual arms.

The Dragon harrumphed.

"I came as soon as I heard you needed someone with . . . my special abilities," the Changeling said. "What can I do you for, Your Lowness?"

The Dragon could have incinerated the Changeling on the spot, but he looked amused. "What else can you do?"

Immediately the Changeling took the form of RHM and put his arm around the Dragon's aide. "It's all in a day's work, sire."

The Dragon raised his eyebrows. "You sound just like him."

"All I have to do is observe someone, and I can change into that person. Or I can pick up cues from their memory." The Changeling treated the Dragon to impressions of several members of his council, including the deceased Dreadwart.

"Splendid," the Dragon said. "This will work nicely."

The Changeling bowed. "I'm pleased to have gained your favor, sire. I saved my best for last."

With a whirl, the Changeling stood face-to-face with the Dragon—*as* the Dragon. The two circled each other, squinting.

RHM blinked and looked on as if he didn't know which was which.

When the Dragon spat fire, the Changeling transformed himself into a stick with a piece of meat sizzling and glowing.

"That was not in the least amusing," the Dragon said.

The Changeling reverted to himself. "Begging your pardon, Your Dragon-ness, but I had to show you my abilities." He held up an index finger. "I have many talents—many of which you still have not seen."

"I will admit that," the Dragon said. "Now to our agreement and the task before you."

The three huddled over their plans. The Changeling asked questions as they studied a map of the kingdom.

"Easy as taking candy from a baby," the Changeling said, transforming himself into a baby in a carriage. He cried as RHM wheeled him from the room.

Watcher awoke when the first
rays of sunlight peeked into
the cave she and the Wormling had
chosen for shelter on their journey
to find the Scribe. They had heard
from townspeople that a man fitting
the description lived near the White
Mountain, and this was the direction
they journeyed now.

The Wormling lay fast asleep, his
eyebrows knitted and cheeks ruddy. He
had grown stronger, and now his arms
tensed as if he were in some battle.

She shook her head. "Keep up the
fight, good Wormling," she whispered
as she slipped out of the cave.

Watcher carried their drinking

gourd in her mouth to bring back some water from the nearby brook for the Wormling. She set it down and lapped at the cool water, letting it refresh her. It was all she could do to resist jumping in.

She had dipped the gourd and stepped away when she noticed a man standing next to a tree along the path to the cave, his back to her. He hadn't been there when she passed . . . or had he? He wore the familiar tunic of the hill people she had grown up with. She stepped closer, studying him. The figure seemed familiar, but she couldn't place him.

"You there," she said softly, her words muffled by the gourd.

When the man turned, Watcher dropped the gourd, and it split on a rock. She rushed to him. "Is it really you? Can it be?"

"Ah, Watcher," the man said, opening his arms wide. "It's been such a long time."

Watcher buried her face in the man's chest as he embraced her. "Bardig," she said. "I can't believe it."

Awakening

Watcher?" Owen said softly as
he sat up. He was alone in the
dark cave, only the glowing embers
from last night's fire giving any light.

It was not strange for Watcher to
wander off. But it had been a while
since she had done that, especially
after their narrow escape from the
Dragon. Watcher had not let Owen
out of her sight.

Owen felt uneasy as he stretched,
and his sword clanged against a rock.
He could not imagine life without the
weapon now. It empowered him and
made him battle ready. He had proved
himself again and again—even surprised

himself against the venomous beasts guarding the book at the castle.

The book.

Pain shot through his chest each time he thought of it. To think of the Dragon in custody of that precious tome . . . Owen vowed to get it back. But how?

"Watcher!" he called, louder now, annoyed that she was not close. It was enough to keep himself safe, let alone having to worry about her.

Owen wandered outside to soaring pine trees and others with white bark and small leaves turning from green to yellow. The whole countryside looked golden with these trees clumped in the midst of the pines. It was beautiful, but with Watcher missing, he couldn't enjoy it.

Owen lumbered down the path, yawning and rubbing his eyes. Finding the broken gourd, he called for Watcher again.

She's probably looking for another gourd. But we have to be going.

Owen knelt by the stream and cupped a hand to the water. It was cool and refreshing. His hair and body felt dirty. For the moment, he was glad that Watcher was gone, because he peeled off his tunic and clothes and plunged in, coming up for air and shaking his hair like a dog. The cold water was invigorating, bringing to mind his life before in the Highlands, as these people called it. Would anyone in *his* world believe him if he returned and told them of this world? That animals could talk? That he plunged into a cold stream after spending the night in a cave? That his sword bore magical powers?

Owen took one last dive before surfacing and wading to the bank. Clouds rolled in, engulfing the sun, and a mist covered the trees. He quickly dried and dressed and strapped on his sword, alert for any sign of Watcher.

As he headed back to the cave via the path, the mist suddenly swallowed the landscape, and the world turned white. Squinting to avoid bumping into something, he gasped.

A hooded specter appeared before him, enshrouded in the mist. "I've been waiting for you, Owen."

That voice. Could it be?

"Oh, it's me all right, young friend." The hood came off, and Owen found himself looking into the face of his mentor.

"Mordecai! How did you find us?"

The man laughed. "It wasn't easy; I can tell you. Where is Watcher?"

Owen frowned. "Off looking for food, I suppose. Come wait in the cave with me."

Mordecai threw his arm around Owen. When they reached the cave, Owen rushed for the spit and tore off what was left of the jargid from the night before, handing it to Mordecai.

Mordecai turned up his nose. "No, thank you. I'm queasy this morning."

"But you love jargid!"

"Oh! I didn't recognize it the way you cooked it." Mordecai accepted the meat and ripped it with his teeth, chuckling. His face shone.

Warmth washed over Owen. "I didn't think I'd ever see you again. How did you get off the island?"

"You underestimate me," Mordecai said. "A little tree cutting and vine lashing, and I had a skiff. The question is not how I got here but how you escaped the Dragon."

"How did you hear about that?"

Mordecai smiled, blackened jargid meat stuck between his teeth. "Tales of the Wormling are flooding the land. You are quite the celebrity, especially after defeating those demon vipers." He touched Owen's sword. "I don't suppose you could have done it without this."

"No," Owen said. "But the best weapon in the world would not have helped without your instruction."

Mordecai rolled his eyes, his thick beard glistening with jargid juice. His lips were like cherries, his eyebrows as bushy as ever. "I didn't have to teach you much."

Owen's heart sank. If Mordecai had heard what happened at the castle, he must have heard about the death of his own son, Qwamay. But it didn't seem so.

Owen moved near the entrance. "Watcher will be so excited to see you. We talk about you every day."

Mordecai tossed the jargid carcass on the coals. "You have a good friend in her, Wormling. I can't wait to see her."

"Uh, Mordecai? There's something I must tell you. Something terrible."

Mordecai furrowed his brow and sat, crossing his ankles. "You haven't lost *The Book of the King*, have you?"

Owen nodded. "I'm afraid the Dragon has it, but awful as that is, I have even worse news."

Mordecai stroked his beard. "I can't imagine, but I'm listening."

"I got into a cell in the castle, believing I was releasing the King's Son."

"You did? And . . ."

"Mordecai, I'm so sorry. The prisoner turned out to be Qwamay."

Mordecai squinted, breathless. "*He's* not the King's Son! He's *my* son! Where is he?"

Owen told him the whole story, except for the fact that the young man had temporarily been in league with the Dragon.

"We escaped with the help of friends, but Qwamay was shot by an archer. By the time we realized it, the wound was too far gone for even the magic of the sword. I'm so sorry, my friend. He died and we buried him."

The news didn't seem to register with Mordecai, and he merely gazed into Owen's eyes.

Owen knelt before him and took one of Mordecai's big hands in his own. "Your son loved you very much."

Finally Mordecai wailed, "My son!" He rose, threw his hands in the air, and pressed his face against the wall of the cave. His crying became a howl, and Owen was sure some demon flyer would hear.

"Oh, Qwamay!" Mordecai moaned, weeping. "I should have come for you long ago." He turned, chin quivering. "Tell me it was a peaceful death."

"It was a courageous death," Owen said, but Mordecai rushed out. Owen followed, noticing that the mist had lifted. The man sat in a bed of brown pine needles, grabbed two handfuls of pinecones, and brought them to his face. Owen had never seen such a hopeless figure.

Where was Watcher when he needed her?

"Mordecai?" Owen said quietly, hands on the big man's shoulders. "I'm sorry, but we're not safe out here."

Mordecai rose slowly and followed Owen back inside, wiping his face and sobbing.

"Can I get you anything?" Owen said gently.

Mordecai shook his head. "It is enough to know that my son spent his last moments with you—that he knew the Wormling had come." He patted Owen on the back. "I'm sure you and your friends were a comfort to him."

"We tried to be. You can be proud of him."

Mordecai took a deep breath. "I'm sure my life confused him."

"I'm sorry?"

"Because I was loyal to the King and then betrayed him." He lifted his eyes to Owen. "Sometimes I think it would have been better to make a truce with the Dragon than to have an all-out fight. No one wins."

"I don't understand."

Mordecai scanned the cave's ceiling. "The book says something about the King knowing the end from the beginning, doesn't it?"

"It is unsearchable," Owen said. "Inexhaustible. It never ends."

"And if the King knows everything, he knew I would fail to protect him and his family. He knew I would slip up, that his Son would be taken, and that all these years would pass before you came onto the scene."

"Which is why I believe the King still loves you and wants you to serve him."

Mordecai waved. "Not my point. My point is that there is so much pain and difficulty, and this cannot be what the King wants. Look what happened when Bardig went up against Dreadwart. He was killed needlessly."

"He gave his life for us."

"But wouldn't it be better for his family if they could have old Bardig around? better to have him when the battle really counted?"

"*The Book of the King* is clear," Owen said. "We are to allow the Dragon no room to reign."

"Yes, but isn't your main purpose to find the King's Son and thereby unite the worlds and create peace? Wouldn't it be best to live to see that happen?"

"I believe it will happen, because I've read it in the book."

6

Mordecai's Vision

"Follow me," Mordecai said, leading Owen above the cave to a switchback path overlooking the countryside. They reached a ledge above the tops of the pines, and the entire valley stretched before them. The stream looked like a pencil-thin line.

Though Owen felt unprotected here, Mordecai's step had lightened.

"Look, Wormling. A beautiful world, isn't it?"

"Almost as beautiful as the island," Owen said.

Mordecai chuckled. "You know, you helped me understand something on the island. Life is worth living. I can't simply cower in the shadows any longer.

I have to get back in the fray. And I would hate to think of not being here for that, not being able to counsel you all the way as you face the forces of darkness."

Owen furrowed his brow. "What do you want me to do?"

"Make a truce with the Dragon, call for peace, and make him swear he will not attack. Think what it could mean! Our people could live in harmony again. You would be worshipped, Wormling."

"It is not my desire to be worshipped, Mordecai."

"Did I say worship? I meant venerated. Lifted up. Praised—but only for your wisdom and insight, which, of course, comes from the King. After all, the book says that peace rules with wisdom."

Owen stared at Mordecai. Gone was the angry man he had known on the island, and in his place stood a man who spoke of peace. But at what price? A truce with his mortal enemy? "On the island, you said there could be no treaty with a prince of lies."

Mordecai shrugged. "Difficult, I'll admit. But think of the advantages. Less death and destruction. More beings who can enjoy life. Makes perfect sense, does it not?"

"Mordecai! The Dragon would never agree to a truce! He would send his demon flyers and—"

"Oh, but he *would* agree," Mordecai said. "He sees strength in you. He has to admire your courage and how far you will go in your quest for the Son. I would be glad to go ahead of you and negotiate this peace."

Owen was thrilled to again be in Mordecai's company, but how could he have so drastically changed his position? Did he really believe a truce would bring peace in the land? Perhaps the loss of his son had clouded his vision. "What would I have to give up in such a truce?"

"Nothing of consequence," Mordecai said. "Just some show of good faith. Perhaps your sword, but nothing of real—"

"My sword?! The Dragon already has *The Book of the King*!"

"Something that shows you are being earnest."

Owen turned away. He loved Mordecai and trusted him, but the man was speaking nonsense. As he stared off, he noticed some sort of animal moving far below beside the stream.

"Pay no attention to the things of the earth," Mordecai said. "They will be here when other things have passed."

" 'Flowers wither and die and the grass disappears,' " Owen said. " 'The King's words are the only things that last.' "

"I suppose. Now, concerning the truce . . ."

Owen suddenly realized the figure below was Watcher. He called out to her just as Mordecai bashed him with a rock, sending him reeling toward the edge. Owen grabbed the root of a tree, but Mordecai was on him, stomping on his hands.

"Mordecai!"

"I could have given you everything you asked for, Wormling! Lands. Power. Authority."

"Those are not yours to give! Nor the Dragon's. Only the King can bestow such. You know that."

"Yes, I know that," Mordecai said, imitating Owen's voice. He bent and hefted an even larger rock. "The King is all-powerful. The King is all-knowing. Well, the King is dead. And so are you."

Mordecai held the stone over Owen's head and let go.

7

Changeling

Owen snapped to reality as the stone dropped toward him. This was not Mordecai but an evil impostor!

Owen struggled to pull himself up but had to let go of a tree root to elude the rock, and he began to slide over the side of the ledge, his body teetering. The cliff angled so steeply that he had to fight his way up or else fall to his death.

"What have you done with Mordecai?" Owen raged, grabbing the root again.

The being mocked him, repeating his words and laughing. "How should I know where he is? Probably back on that island eating the disgusting meat you fed me." The impostor bent to pick up another rock as Owen fought to hang on.

"The Dragon sent you?" Owen said.

"Oh, you're a genius, you are. Of course the Dragon sent me. I convinced him I could talk sense into you, but obviously Wormlings are more worm than brain."

Hundreds of feet below, Owen saw Watcher move into the open, struggling to free herself from constraints. He felt alone, as if the arm in the night, his unseen protector, had left him.

With another gigantic rock hoisted over his head, the impostor smiled. "Enjoy the view while it lasts."

"A word, if you please," Owen said. "You are good. You had me believing you were my friend."

"I do pride myself on my work. It pains me to have to resort to violence when a simple agreement would have saved so many lives. But you would not listen." The impostor inched closer but not close enough so Owen could reach his leg.

Owen was slipping, and strength ebbed from him as he hung there.

"Sad," the impostor said. "Anything you'd like to say before you smash what little brains you have on the rocks down there?"

"Just one word."

"I can grant that."

"Sword!"

The impostor smirked, clearly confused. "Whatever. Have a nice fall—and a wonderful spring. Good-bye, Wormling."

A silver object flew from the cave, turning golden and twinkling in the light. Before the impostor could drop the rock, Owen lurched, reached high to catch the sword, and in one motion swung it toward the impostor, catching him just above the ankle.

The impostor yelped and fell back, the rock thudding behind him. His boot had been sliced through, and blood spurted.

Owen stuck the sword in the earth and used it to pull himself up as the impostor writhed.

"Think a little flesh wound will stop me?" the being yelled. He scooted backward, pushing with his good foot, and stopped against a wall of rock.

Owen watched the impostor's eyes roll back in his head, the beard and bushy eyebrows of Mordecai sink into his face, and the being change into a scaly, green gecko with a slithering tongue and his foot restored.

As the impostor tried to skitter away, Owen plunged the sword through his tail, trapping him.

The animal squealed. "Why are you doing this?"

"You tried to kill me!" Owen said.

"I wouldn't have gone through with it. Besides, I was only following orders. Now release me."

Owen used his tunic to wrap the animal and carry it, squirming and wriggling, down the mountain. "Hold still or I'll slice you in two," Owen said.

The gecko went suddenly rigid.

As soon as Owen reached Watcher, he cut her gag and bindings.

"He's a Changeling," she said, gasping. "Came to me in the form of Bardig."

"But I didn't hurt you, did I?" the Changeling whined. "See, Wormling, I didn't—"

"Quiet," Owen said with authority. He carried the Changeling to the cave and tied him up.

"The demon flyers will be near," Watcher said. "We should leave."

"Not until we find out what he knows," Owen said.

But the Changeling quickly turned into a snake and was crawling away when Owen again used his sword to pin him to the ground.

"Return to your original form," Owen said, "and I'll remove my sword."

"And whom would you prefer?" the Changeling said, turning back into Bardig. "An old friend?" He rolled his eyes again. "Maybe a competitor?" Now he was Connor, Bardig's son.

"Stop it!" Owen said.

The Changeling smiled. "Someone more regal?" With a nod, he was the Queen, shoulders back, wearing a dress with puffed sleeves. "I'm rather enjoying this, Wormling."

Watcher growled, and Owen raised his sword. "Be careful, Changeling."

But the creature had done it again. "Perhaps someone from your past." And there stood Owen's father. "So nice to see you again, Son."

Owen nearly dropped his sword. "How could you know about . . . ?"

"I'm just getting started." Next he was Gordan Kalb, the bully at Owen's school. Then Clara Secrest, the pretty girl Owen had taken to a movie.

Owen stared, dumbfounded. When the Changeling turned into his young friend Constance, Owen held up his sword. "Stop or I'll have to hurt you."

The Changeling turned back into the gecko and crossed his stubby arms. "Satisfied?"

"How do you know the people in my world?"

The Changeling smiled. "Certain memories are stronger than others. I simply tap into yours."

"I need to know something. Does the Dragon know where the King's Son is?"

"And why should I tell you?"

"Because my weapon is sharp."

"Good reason." The Changeling crossed his gecko legs. "I hear he has escaped."

Watcher nudged Owen, but he shook her off. "Can you become the Son? Right now?"

"I've never seen him, but . . ." He closed his eyes and turned into a dark-haired hunk, strong as an ox, face chiseled from stone.

"Is that him?" Owen said.

"It's your perception, as I suppose you've never laid eyes on him either." The Changeling leaned forward, hair changing to brown, nose growing bulbous, and shrinking several inches. "This is *her* perception."

"Really," Owen said.

Watcher made a face. "It's just the way I thought he would look," she said.

Owen turned back to the Changeling. "Did the Dragon have a book?"

The Changeling studied his fingernails. "*The Book of the King*. He was poring over it, unable to make sense of it as far as I could tell. Fire, brimstone, destruction, the end of the world, blah, blah, blah. Sounded dreadful. I have enough trouble with what *is* without worrying what *might* be."

"What else did he talk about?" Owen said.

The Changeling looked around the cave.

"Don't worry," Watcher said. "No invisibles here."

"Well, you can't blame me for being careful. You know what the Dragon would do if he knew I was giving you information rather than bringing you back to the castle? Can you say 'toasted Changeling'?"

"You were supposed to take me there?"

"And broker a truce between you two. I try to be a bit more subtle."

"They thought *you* were the best way to get to me?"

"Don't act so surprised. As you said, I'm good."

Watcher moved closer to Owen. "Which means they're afraid of you. Afraid of your power."

The Changeling frowned. "I don't know about that, but they're upset about something missing from that musty old book."

"Missing?" Watcher said.

"The Dragon was all in a tizzy about some missing chapters and how they've looked for them. You'd think the fate of the world hung on those pages."

Something passed between Owen and Watcher.

Quickly Owen turned back to the Changeling. "Can you tell what we're thinking or just who we're thinking about?"

The Changeling rolled his eyes. "Why would I want to read your minds? Even if I could, I wouldn't waste my time."

"He's lying," Watcher said.

"How dare you!"

"This is why he was sent, why he's cooperating. He wants to read our minds and tell the Dragon."

"If I could read your mind, I would have known you were going to think that and changed the subject. Maybe *you* can read *my* mind." The Changeling sighed and waved. "Think what you will. I'm done talking. It does me no good to be of service to your side or the Dragon's." He put a hand to his forehead. "I'm simply alone in the world."

Owen pulled Watcher to the other side of the cave. "We can't let him go back to the Dragon. We'll have to take him with us."

"What? And alert every demon flyer between here and the invisible kingdom?"

"What choice do we have, Watcher?"

"Kill him."

Owen tilted his head. "And you're the sensitive, loving one?"

"Doesn't the book say something about rooting out the enemies of the King and destroying them utterly?"

Owen closed his eyes and recalled a passage. " 'There is no middle ground. Either you are for the King or you are against him.' "

"Exactly. And if this one—"

"He's an opportunist," Owen said. "Someone who takes advantage of both sides. He's harmless."

"How can someone the Dragon trusts be harmless? Everything in me says we cannot let him report to the enemy—"

"All right," Owen said, smiling. "We'll take him with us and keep him out of sight. He can turn into a donkey, and I'll ride him. Better still, a motorcycle."

"What's a motorcycle?"

8

Decisions

The Changeling bounced along on Owen's shoulders, bound and gagged and taking the form of Starbuck, Erol's small son. He seemed disgruntled to have to become such a lowly creature, but Owen said, "Morph into one more being, and I'll run my sword through your heart."

The three moved in the shadows of pine trees down a path that meandered into a plain. To the west loomed the stately and majestic White Mountain. Watcher grazed on grains, and Owen offered some to the Changeling.

"No, thanks," he said. "I can't abide the chaff."

As the sun beat down, the

Changeling moaned. They finally stopped in the shade of an outcropping of rocks and drank from their ration of water.

"You're giving him *our* water?" Watcher said to Owen.

"It would be cruel to let him dehydrate."

"And cruelty does not become the Wormling," the Changeling said. "The Wormling is kind and considerate and is here to set the captive free . . ."

Owen glared at the Changeling, gripping the hilt of his sword.

". . . and he has a sharp sword that he knows how to use, and the captive will now be quiet."

"A word with you," Watcher whispered after Owen checked the Changeling's bindings again. They stepped away a few paces. "He's slowing us. Dividing us. The book says that two who are divided cannot walk a straight path."

Owen nodded. "But this is my decision, not yours."

"And you're wrong. You should have destroyed him back at the cave. They would never have found him."

"And we wouldn't know what the Dragon thinks—"

"We still don't," she said. "We know only what he tells us, and that could be a plot by the evil one as well."

"You want me to run my sword through him? Cold-blooded murder?"

"Your quest is to find the King's Son, not care for some traitor. . . ." Watcher's voice trailed off. "Oh no. Look."

The rope that had secured the Changeling lay on the ground, knotted and limp next to the gag. Owen found footprints in the sand that ended at the rock pile. "Happy now, Watcher? We're rid of him."

"I am not happy," she said. "And I doubt we are rid of him or those he consorts with."

9
Questions in the Night

O wen and Watcher quickly gathered their things and stayed close to darkened forest trails the rest of the day until they found a cavern in a distant hill. Watcher fell asleep quickly, but Owen tossed and turned, wondering what the Changeling might tell the Dragon. Had he been able to read their thoughts? Would Owen's decision to let him live prove disastrous?

Owen finally dozed, and when both awakened just before sundown, they dined on berries and nuts and soon set out again. Watcher said she was using the White Mountain as orientation to guide them toward Vezlev, a populated village on the other side of the Amoyn Valley where they hoped to find the Scribe.

They forded a stream, then followed it down the hillside, replenishing their water supply. Watcher seemed unusually quiet.

"All right," Owen said. "You were right. I should have killed the Changeling while I had the chance. Feel better?"

Watcher gave him a pained look. "Being right isn't the point."

"Then what is?"

She took a drink and frowned. "The humans from the other world that the Changeling turned into. Who were they?"

"The first was my father. For a second I thought it was actually him."

"Was he nice?"

"I suppose. He provided for me. Let me read. He was not as loving as Erol and his clan with their children, but you can't have everything."

"Your voice has pain in it."

"You can't change your parents. Or their actions." Owen explained what had happened at the bookstore before he began his journey. Watcher was right. The memory was painful.

"And who were the others?" Watcher asked.

"The second was a bully who tried to hurt me."

"And the girl?"

"Constance? Just a child I know from—"

"No, the other. The older, pretty one."

Owen blushed and looked away. "A friend. Clara."

"You have special feelings for her?"

Owen glanced back at Watcher. "Why all these questions?"

"I want to know. I don't think it's fair for you to hide things from me. If we're to be comrades in this fight—"

"Fair? There's plenty you don't know about me, Watcher, and I about you. It doesn't mean I'm hiding anything. Where did you get that notion?"

Watcher turned and resumed walking.

"Come, come, Watcher. If we're spilling all our secrets, tell me how that idea came to you." Owen knew that if Watcher lied, she would permanently lose her powers. "Tell me where this distrust comes from."

"The Dragon," Watcher said, the fur on her chin trembling and her eyes filling.

Owen averted his gaze, remembering how frightened she had been in the castle, bound to a chair, vulnerable and alone. Suddenly he felt pity for her. "What did he say to you?"

"The Dragon told me your heart belonged to someone in the other world and that you didn't want me to know."

"If I was in love with someone, why wouldn't I want you to know?"

"I'm just telling you what he said."

What was the Dragon up to, planting this doubt in Watcher's mind? Owen stopped and faced her. "He was trying to trick you. Why would something like this trouble you?"

Watcher looked up, eyes wide. "Please. No more questions."

10

More Questions

The Amoyn Valley lay in the shadow of the White Mountain, a day's journey away. At this time of year, the forests surrounding it blazed with color, and the swollen river through the valley carried the last of the melting snow from the mountain. Soon the valley would be covered white and stay that way until the spring thaw.

Deep in the night, Watcher cut across a swampy area with Owen close behind. He hated getting his feet wet. It took his socks a long time to dry, so he tried finding a dry route. But he stepped in even deeper holes, making his foul mood much worse.

Then Owen spotted firelight on the horizon, which heartened him. He ran in his soggy shoes, squishing as he went.

"Wait!" Watcher whispered. "It may be the enemy."

"Here?" Owen said, pulling up. "Wouldn't you have sensed them by now?"

"I sense something but not a demon flyer or anything like it. I sense anger and pain and determination."

"That and dry feet sound too good to pass up. Come on." Owen stuck a wet sock on the end of his sword as a sign of friendship (at least hoping someone would interpret it that way).

But a sentry sounded an alarm. Troops came running, bleary-eyed, but when they saw it was just a teen boy and a Watcher, they returned to their tents.

Owen asked the sentry if they could use one of the campfires to dry out until morning.

"You'll have to ask our leader."

"Why do you burn fires in the open?" Watcher said. "Are you not afraid of an attack?"

"Orders of our leader," he said, leading them toward a large tent.

Along the way Owen noticed that these Lowland warriors looked much like the hill people he had first come to live with. Their clothing was cheap sackcloth and their shoes little more than pieces of leather or jargid skins. Owen felt guilty about complaining of wet socks.

Watcher whispered, "There's something here I don't like. We should leave."

"These are good people," Owen said. "What could possibly be wrong?"

Beside the leader's tent stood a strange weapon, and the man's tethered horse bore a blanket embroidered with a coat of arms.

"I've seen that somewhere," Owen muttered.

The tent flap opened, and Owen's mouth dropped.

11
Unpleasant Reunion

Connor, son of Bardig, stepped out of the tent, his hair flickering golden in the firelight. He shot a double take at Owen, who held a wet sock in one hand and a sword in the other. Connor pulled his sword and stepped back.

Owen held up the sock. "We mean you no harm. We just wanted to warm ourselves." He looked at Watcher. "We should be going."

"I'm sorry," Watcher muttered. "Was that an echo?"

"Stand your ground!" Connor spat, raising his sword to Owen's neck.

Swords clanged around them as warriors emerged from their tents. "Now raise your weapon."

Owen stuffed his sock in a pocket. "I do not wish to fight you, Connor. I only regret I could not do more for your father—"

"You never finished your duel," a young man said. "The flood washed us away. How convenient for you."

"I warned you of the flood," Watcher said, "but you wouldn't listen."

The young man swung his sword at Watcher's neck.

But another sword intercepted it and held it there. The Sword of the Wormling. "Do not test me," Owen said evenly.

"Well, Gunnar," Connor said, "you've managed to raise the ire of the Wormling. Seize the Watcher."

And the fight began. Owen flicked Gunnar's sword from his hands. Connor advanced, but Owen fought him back, kicking Gunnar in the chest as he tried to grab Watcher. She ran behind a tent, shouting for Owen to follow, kicking at captors who seemed to pour from every tent.

Owen and Connor were quickly surrounded by cheering, clapping spectators, every one rooting for the home team.

Connor lunged and thrust his sword straight at Owen's chest.

Owen deftly parried and pushed Connor back.

"So the rumors are true?" Connor asked. "You trained with Mordecai. Did the traitor give you that stolen sword?"

Owen blocked another stab and forced Connor back again. "He is no traitor, and this is the Sword of the Wormling."

Watcher yelped as three men pulled her to the ground, diverting Owen's attention. Connor moved in for the kill, but Owen dropped to the ground and tripped him. Connor was quickly up, but Owen could see he could hardly breathe.

"Let go of me!" Watcher yelled.

"You might want to watch—"

"Ow!" one man said, limping away.

"—her back legs," Owen said.

"Oof," another said, falling.

"Her front legs are powerful too. The only other thing—"

"Whoa!" a man called, flying into a tent.

"—is her head butt. You're going to be sore in the morning."

Watcher moved to Owen's side, so close that he could feel her breath. He stared at Connor as the entire camp surrounded them. "Fine then," Owen said. "I'll dry my socks somewhere else."

Connor shook his head. "Not so fast, Wormling."

Connor rushed him, and the clang of swords rang through the countryside. Owen anticipated Connor's every move and effortlessly fended him off. When Connor was backed up against the crowd, another sword came out, and Owen blocked it. As he swung to counter Connor's next thrust, his blade sliced Connor's ear clean, and it plopped in the dirt.

Connor went down, holding his head.

Gunnar rushed Owen from behind.

"Stop!" Owen said, clanging swords with him. "I'm not going to hurt Connor." He picked up the ear, poured water over it from a cup, and reached for Connor.

The man recoiled. "You mock me?"

"Let him help you," Watcher said.

Owen placed the ear back and raised his sword, making Connor jerk away again. "Just trust me," Owen said quietly.

When the sword gently touched the side of Connor's head, sweat and water trickled onto it, creating a fine, white mist. Owen stood, and the men gasped. The ear had been restored.

"He's a miracle worker," someone said.

"It's magic," Gunnar said. "The Dragon's doing."

"I would use the Dragon's power to cure an enemy of the Dragon?" Owen said.

"It's not the Wormling at all," another said, eyeing Owen closely. "It's the Dragon himself, dressed as a Wormling."

"Then why haven't I consumed you?" Owen said, laughing. "I honor you who dare to fight him, though, for he is a worthy foe."

Connor stood. "You compliment him?"

"I just said he was a worthy foe, but he will be defeated. Of that you can be sure."

Connor touched his ear and motioned Owen and Watcher into his tent.

Owen took off a shoe and hopped about the circle with his socks in his hands. "Would you mind terribly if I hung these near the fire?"

A small lamp gave off heat in the center of the tent, and Watcher lay down next to it. Owen sat on animal skins, his bare feet near the lamp.

"What brings you to our battle line, Wormling?" Connor said.

"You're waiting for a battle? Your fires are bright enough to attract many enemies."

"I've assembled warriors from several provinces. We have enough to make an interesting fight."

"You have enough to bloody this field, Connor. But it's not time. When the Son returns—"

"You speak of the King's Son often. I think it's a convenient excuse."

"The Son is the key to any battle against the Dragon. Without him, you would be fighting not only the Dragon but the prophecy as well."

Connor smirked and shook his head. "The prophecy! I hear you let this book that was so important to you fall into the hands of the mortal enemy of the King. Doesn't that put your job as a Wormling in danger?"

Watcher sat up. "You have no idea how the Wormling fought to get the book back—or of his fight in the Castle of the Pines."

"The King's castle? A strange place to find the Son; it's been abandoned so long."

"The prophecy is clear," Owen said. "The Dragon will be defeated but not before the Son returns. He will lead you into battle, and not until then can you succeed. You'll fight only in your own strength."

Connor took a bite of fruit and spit out a seed. "Do you know how long we've waited, suffered under the talons of that Dragon? Already we are winning. We decimated a raiding party of vaxors two days ago."

"Vaxors?" Owen said.

"Repulsive," Watcher said. "They fight with axes and clubs."

"Just because you defeated these—whatever you call them," Owen said, "doesn't mean you should take up *this* battle."

"I've heard of the Wormling and the prophecies all my life.

I've been told to sit and wait, and I've watched my country-men obey like sheep, running and hiding and hoping we would survive each attack by the Dragon. I will run no more."

"You will die."

"At least I will have done something instead of just talk-ing about what *might* be someday. Women talk. Children tell stories. Men *fight*."

"Do not ridicule your women," Owen said. "They are strong in spirit and will fight when the time comes. And don't belittle the stories of children or their love of those stories. It is their innocence and purity the Dragon hates the most. And the King loves the most. In this battle, the King can use any and all who wish to follow him."

"This book of yours—does it say such things?" Connor asked.

Owen nodded. "Some passages lift the heart like nothing else in the world. Others give perspective, let you know that no one is perfect, that all of us make mistakes and are tar-nished by our choices."

Connor shook his head. "It should be called *The Book of Jabber*. We need less babbling and more action. If you really believe that book, act. Join us and fight."

"No," Owen said, "that's the point. The fight is not *yours*, Connor. The fight is *his*. And he will win the battle. But we have to align ourselves with his timetable, with his plans."

"The King?" Connor said. "I'd say his timetable has already run out, wouldn't you? He's left us. And he's not coming back."

"Connor, listen—"

"No. The King left a long time ago. Turned tail and ran. Left us at the mercy of the Dragon. And we've been told all this time that we simply have to wait, that fighting would be futile, that we have no say. Well, I'm not going to just sit and take whatever the Dragon dishes out." Connor threw his fruit on the floor with a splat. "Enough of my countrymen have been dragged away in service to this beast. If I die, I die. But I will not sit by while more are slaughtered or made slaves."

Owen's heart broke for Connor. With emotion in his voice, he said, "I have met your Queen. Her strength and beauty are great, and though she serves in a lowly place, she has not let that bring her low. I too want to slay every enemy of the King. But this is not the time. It would be suicide to taunt the Dragon now."

Connor shook his head. "Your words are well chosen and may stir others, but my father lies under the earth because of those words."

Owen sat up. "Many will fight with us. Watcher and I have seen courage from those the King called and touched. But the time is not yet right."

Connor moved to the entrance and opened the flap, peering out at the encampment. "When?"

"You are courageous and determined," Owen said. "But this battle, unless waged in the strength of the King, will fail."

"At least we will die trying."

Watcher's voice rang out. "So you're really not interested in winning."

"You have no idea—"

"You would rather have a statue in your honor placed on this field than to have true victory."

"How dare you!"

"'To Connor, the brave,'" Watcher said, pointing a hoof to an imaginary statue. "'And to those who followed him to their deaths. Hail the courageous leader who fought his own battle.'"

Connor unsheathed his sword and pressed it against her neck, his hand shaking.

Owen gently pushed the sword away.

"Don't you see?" Watcher said. "This is what the Dragon wants. He divides us so that he can conquer. If we unite, at the right time, we'll win."

Connor sat and sighed. "See how blindly you follow without asking questions?"

"I have questions," Owen said, "but my faith in the King and his Son outweighs my doubts."

Connor sneered. "I pity you."

13

Call to Arms

While Owen retrieved his toasty shoes and socks, Watcher found a stable boy who knew the directions to the village of Vezlev.

"I'm from Yuhrmer," the boy said, "but I had to go through Vezlev to get here. Why are you going there?"

Watcher explained.

"I have heard of such a man, but he does not live in Vezlev. His home is in Yodom."

Watcher nodded excitedly as she listened to the directions to the small village. She couldn't wait to tell the Wormling what she'd learned, but the boy seemed to want to talk.

"I really liked how you and the Wormling fought," the lad said. "I wish

I could go with you. I mean, I want to fight the Dragon and see his demon flyers fall too."

"One day you may be a warrior, son," Watcher said, "but now your job is tending horses. An army cannot win without strong animals, you know."

"I would rather fight like you and the Wormling."

"Each task is important. Do you think being a Watcher was much fun, especially all those years waiting?"

He grinned. "That would be even more boring than caring for horses."

"We are nothing on our own—none of us. But the King's authority makes us warriors. *The Book of the King* says, 'Whoever is faithful in a little will be given much more.' "

The boy beamed. "Would the Wormling accept a gift?"

"We are not able to carry much."

"This would help. I was given a colt some time ago, but he's grown too large for me to ride. I'm sure the Wormling could use him."

Watcher smiled. How many times had she wished the Wormling could walk as fast and long as she? But how could they accept such a gift? "It is a wonderful gesture, but we could not—"

"I insist," the boy said, untying the horse. It had patches of brown and white and a gentle face. "My contribution to the cause."

Owen was happy to hear the news about the Scribe's where-abouts, but he eyed the horse warily. He had learned to swim by being thrown into the water by Mordecai, and he supposed he could learn to ride simply by getting on. At first it felt awkward, the horse shifting back and forth, but with Watcher's instructions and the fact that the horse seemed to sense Owen's unease, he rode toward the sunrise.

No longer concerned about demon flyers, since they figured to be more interested in Connor's army, Owen and Watcher moved into the open, down to the river that ran past the battle line. They followed to an arroyo, then north toward the White Mountain.

"You sure about these directions?" Owen said.

"The stable boy seemed quite sure," Watcher said.

They had traveled only an hour when black clouds rolled in behind them. Owen suggested they find shelter, but Watcher said, "Those are not storm clouds."

"There's lightning behind us. Of course it's a storm."

"No," Watcher said. "The battle has begun."

Owen turned around and urged his horse faster, hanging on tight to the reins. Watcher ran ahead, dust swirling behind her hooves. She turned to check on him, but Owen waved her on.

She disappeared over the horizon, then returned less than half an hour later, panting. "Scythe flyers descending . . . some have fallen . . . and demon flyers, too!"

"Killed?" Owen said.

"I think so. . . ." Watcher pointed toward the White Mountain. "Also a small band of men heading north." She turned and hurried back over the hill.

Owen's mind raced. Had he misread the prophecy? Should he have helped this group and defeated some of the Dragon's warriors?

Owen dismounted at the first dead scythe flyer, whose head was buried in the earth. He marveled at the thickness of the skin and sharpness of the tail. He couldn't understand how Connor and his men had killed it until he found a stake sticking in its belly.

He tied his horse to a tree and hurried toward the field. A weird contraption—a catapult with a wooden pole attached to the front—sat near the front line. Watcher explained that Connor had an exploding spear that had brought down several scythe flyers and scared off the demon flyers.

"Any warriors hurt?"

Watcher nodded. "In those tents. They put warriors in front to draw the flyers in, then shot them as they passed."

Owen hurried past a man shouting for reinforcements.

"Are you here to join us, Wormling?" the man asked.

Owen didn't answer. He continued running for the tents. What he saw there turned his stomach. Some of the men were missing arms or legs. He couldn't believe Connor had used them as bait.

A man in a white shirt moved among them, checking wounds.

Owen approached, drawing his sword.

"These will live," White Shirt said. "Don't end their suffering. The next tent has men who could be put out of their misery."

Owen went from cot to cot, touching deep gashes with the blade, healing them instantly. Some had been wounded too long and he couldn't help, but many stood, restored.

Watcher rushed inside and told Owen to come quickly. He finished reattaching an arm, and the man hugged him with both hands, joyous. "Thank you, Wormling."

Outside, Watcher said, "Hurry to the field."

Owen followed her, stepping over trenches where scythe flyers had dragged their tails several feet deep. At the top of a knoll, the young boy who had given Owen his horse lay.

Owen knelt. "What are you doing out here in the open?"

"I wanted to help. When the scythe flyers saw me, they had to get extra close to the ground."

Owen examined the boy's stomach. "How long have you been here?"

"They said there was no hope."

Owen held his sword to the wound. But as with Qwamay, it was no use. He had been wounded too long without the Sword's power. Owen removed his tunic and placed it under the boy's head.

"I'm scared to die, Wormling, sir," the boy said, choking.

"Do not be afraid," Owen said, grasping his hand. "This is not the end. We who are faithful to the King will meet again."

"How do you know? How can you be sure?"

" 'There is coming a time of renewal and rebirth. Those who die will live again and serve the King with gladness.' "

The boy's hand fell limp.

All Owen's life he had been moved by the plight of those younger than himself. Children bullied, treated unkindly by teachers, insulted by shop owners. But never had he been so incensed by another's pain.

The dark sky reminded him of the Dragon's pursuit—his hideous face twisted with evil. *He* had caused this death, and that truth burned in Owen's heart. But it was also Connor who had allowed the innocent boy to join them.

Owen gritted his teeth and strode back toward the front line.

14

Taken

W here is Connor?" Owen yelled, voice full of emotion.

Those on the front line simply looked at him with the vacant eyes of the defeated. Gunnar pushed through and stood by one of the strange weapons.

"Wounded?" Owen said. "Killed?"

Gunnar's jaw was set. "Connor is not here."

"Where then?"

Watcher screamed, "Incoming!"

The fighters took their places, some moving into the field as decoys while others manned the weapons.

"Tell us when the invisibles are near, Watcher," Gunnar said. "Please."

She closed her eyes, the hair on her back standing straight, a foreleg toward the sky. "There. Three in the lead—one in front, two close behind."

"And four scythe flyers," Owen said. "We're no match for these."

"Stand your ground, Wormling," Gunnar said.

"You'll get more of your men killed," Owen said. "Why isn't Connor here if he's so committed to this fight?"

"Almost here," Watcher said, still pointing.

Owen held his sword behind his head.

"Now!" Watcher shouted.

Something like fireworks exploded beside Owen, and three sharpened poles hurtled into the air like missiles.

"They're too high!" someone shouted. "They're not attacking!"

The poles reached their apexes, then fell harmlessly as the scythe flyers flew around them.

"Why aren't they attacking?" Watcher said.

Owen sheathed his sword. "They're after something else." He turned to Gunnar. "Where is Connor?"

With a sheepish look, Gunnar said, "His plan was to stage this battle, then steal away to the White Mountain to rescue our friends. Several from our group have been taken there—"

"This was all a show? a ruse to get them to attack?" Owen looked back to where the stable boy lay, then to the tents of the wounded. "He would have given up all these? And Watcher and me?"

"His wife was among those taken. We didn't anticipate this many deaths."

The demon flyers screeched in the distance; then the scythe flyers plummeted. They were mere specks on the horizon, but Owen could see them picking people from the ground and carrying them toward the White Mountain.

"Gather your wounded, Gunnar, and get them to safety. Those flyers will return. And you'll be lucky if they don't make slaves of the lot of you."

15

Decision

To Owen's surprise, that evening he found Watcher standing over the stable boy's grave, whispering tearfully, "'May the King keep you and cause his face to shine upon you and give you peace in the valley of eternity.'"

"Where did you learn that?" Owen said.

"Bardig," she said. "Long ago. He told me the King himself grieves every death, but special in his sight is a child. How can the Dragon delight in the death of one so young?"

Owen, who realized he had grown since coming to the Lowlands, bent to face Watcher. "You encountered the

Dragon and lived to tell about it. You know he will stop at nothing to overthrow the King."

"Which may happen."

"Don't even think that."

Watcher shuddered. "But the Dragon and the Changeling act as if the King is dead."

"Watcher, trust me. With everything in me I know the King lives."

"And his Son?"

Owen looked away.

"See? There is doubt even in you."

"I worry about the Son. But the way the Dragon put a decoy in the dungeon and rewarded Qwamay for posing as the Son leads me to believe the true Son is alive."

Watcher traced something in the dirt, then looked up. "And if we never find him?"

"We will."

"Why can't the King help us? Why must we travel so far and struggle for every morsel of hope?"

"I have asked the same. Why did I have to come here? Why should a Wormling be employed in this search at all? Why not just let the King's Son rise and fight? But it has been worth it to spend time in *The Book of the King* and learn about the King's heart. He is not far from us, Watcher. I believe he is closer than we think. And victory is not far either."

Gunnar and a few of his men interrupted them, thrusting their swords deep into the earth. "We have decided to attempt a rescue," Gunnar said. "Come and bring your Watcher. She can warn us of impending attacks."

Owen pursed his lips. "I tried to talk Connor out of this. I didn't know it was a rescue attempt. Why he didn't tell me is a mystery—"

"He didn't trust you," Gunnar said. "He blames you for what happened to his father."

Owen nodded. "Perhaps one day he'll know the truth. Right now, Watcher and I must continue our quest for the Son."

"You don't care that Connor could be killed?"

"He made his choice. After we've found the Son, we can try to rescue Connor from the White Mountain or wherever the Dragon takes him. I pray he's not killed."

Gunnar shook his head. "Praying is just words. Action counts."

"Action without the blessing of the King is mere exercise." Owen drew closer. "Align yourself with him, yield your strength to his, and he will use you. That's the best way to help your people and Connor."

"Tempting," Gunnar said. "But you leave before a fight is finished. You abandon people and allow them to die. We will try to rescue Connor. If we die, at least we tried."

"I wish you well," Owen said. "And as I say, I will be the first to help once we have found the Son."

Gunnar spat, "Don't bother."

16

The Village

Getting past the White Mountain was difficult, not only because of the terrain but also because Owen felt a tug to help Gunnar.

Watcher asked Owen why saving the children of Erol in the Badlands was any different from this.

"The children were innocent. They didn't choose to go to the mines."

"Neither did Connor's wife and the others. Connor was only trying to do what you did for Erol's clan."

"You argue well," Owen said. "I hate seeing people in such pain, but the real way to help them—and everyone in the Lowlands—is to find the Son and follow the King's words."

☀

Over the next two days, Watcher warned Owen any time invisible scouts drew near. Owen dutifully followed her to safety, but he wished he could slice those pesky creatures in two.

Finally, after walking all night, they reached a range overlooking the village of Yuhrmer.

"Why stop here?" Owen said. "The Scribe lives in Yodom."

"I thought we might eat here and rest."

"How much farther to Yodom?"

Watcher pointed. "Another night's journey. But, Wormling, this is also where the woman lives. The one whose picture is in your backpack."

Owen recalled Watcher having seen the picture of his mother. "I thought you barely traveled from your mountain. How would you have seen this woman?"

Watcher smiled. "Before the Dragon forbade travel, Bardig took me with him when I was a youngling. There was a fair in Zior. People set up booths and tents where they sold the most wonderful fruit and plants and baked goods. And there were games that kept me laughing, just watching the old ones try to win."

"A carnival," Owen said. "That's what we call that in the Highlands."

"Anyway, one booth from Yuhrmer bore the most beautiful bedcovers I had ever seen. Delicate cloth so soft and silky that I didn't think they would even let me touch it. But a kind lady there held it up to my face."

"The lady who looks like my mother?"

Watcher nodded.

✦✦✦

When Owen and Watcher arrived in Yuhrmer, Owen noticed that most of the homes were made of logs, topped with thatched roofs. One, perched slightly above the village, was made of stone, and its wide chimney belched smoke. The pleasing aroma drifting down the hillside reminded Owen of the bakery near his house.

As often happens in small towns, children were the first to meet the strangers, leaving a game played with sticks and a crude ball. The children in Owen's world were driven to soccer practice wearing expensive shoes and played with the best equipment. These kids slapped at a roll of yarn and scurried in the dirt with bare feet. Still they giggled and seemed to be having just as much fun.

Despite the children's worn clothes, their faces were round and they seemed well fed. The girls wore their hair in braids. The boys also had longish hair. Soon Owen and Watcher were surrounded by staring children with dirty hands and faces.

"You look funny," one said, pointing at Owen.

"Stop it, Thomas," an older girl said. Owen figured this was Thomas's sister. "It's not polite to point."

Thomas lowered his finger and scrunched up his face. "He does look funny, though. He's too small to be carrying a big sword. Where'd you get that?"

Owen laughed and pulled it from his scabbard. "It was a gift from a friend." He let Thomas feel its weight, then had to let each child have a turn.

Watcher pawed at the ground as if ready to keep moving, but Owen took off his backpack. The children crowded closer, peering in. The picture of his mother was water damaged and ripped, but it was still clear enough to show the kids. "Have you ever seen her?"

"That's Drushka," a girl said. "At least, I think it is."

Several nodded. "She lives in the bread house—the one with all the stones."

The children guided them to the house. Owen felt uneasy as he climbed the steps. He had been told that his mother had died the day he was born. He had assumed this was why his father was distant and didn't show affection. Owen couldn't blame him. If he had truly loved the woman, and if she'd died giving birth to Owen, that would explain a lot.

But his father had given him information about his mother just before he traveled to the Lowlands—a book of pictures

that included her. Could she still be alive? And could the
woman inside this house be his actual mother?

"Knock," Watcher said. "What's wrong?"

"Well, what do I say? 'Hello, I'm your son, the Wormling'?"

"Wormling?" a child squealed behind them. "He said he
was the Wormling."

Watcher rolled her eyes. "Great, tell everybody."

Owen tapped lightly on the heavy wooden door.

17

The Conversation

Owen felt his face blanch when a woman opened the door, and he worried he might keel over. This was the woman in his picture. She was larger, perhaps, her face fuller and shiny. But she was still beautiful, with dark hair covered by a shawl and a dress nearly reaching her ankles. Her skin was pale, as if she spent too much time in the dark.

"Miss Drushka?" Watcher said.

"Yes," she said with the hint of an accent. "Call me Drushka."

"My friend here thinks he may know you from somewhere. May we come in?"

Drushka wiped her doughy hands on

her apron and stared at Owen. Then she looked past them. "You children leave these two alone. Go and play!"

She ushered Owen and Watcher into the huge kitchen, where she was baking bread. The smell made Owen's mouth water.

"I met you at the fair in Zior years ago," Watcher said. "You let me touch the soft fabric."

"I remember," Drushka said. "Would you like a crimrose? They're fresh from the fire." The woman produced two steaming pastries.

Owen closed his eyes as he took a bite. "This is like a croissant back home. So flaky and soft, it nearly melts in your mouth."

"And where is home?" Drushka said.

"Watcher here is from the hill country, but I'm actually from the Highlands. I'm a Wormling."

Drushka locked her eyes on Owen.

He pulled a worn book from his backpack, its pages crumpled and warped from moisture. Drushka flipped through it, scanning the pictures until she came to one that made her cover her mouth. Owen handed her another—the one he had shown the children. Drushka ran her fingers over it like a child with a new doll.

"Is that you?" Owen said.

She looked overwhelmed. "Where did you get this?"

"From my father. He runs a bookstore in the Highlands. Our name is Reeder."

"He can read," Watcher said. "He even knows much of *The Book of the King*."

The very mention of the sacred book seemed to startle the woman.

Owen said, "Do you have a child?"

Tears came to Drushka's eyes. "A son."

18

Drushka's Story

Owen wanted to rush to Drushka
and embrace her, so sure was he
that she was his mother.

But she turned away and her shoulders shook. "My son was taken long
ago," she managed, weeping.

Owen's heart leaped. "How long
ago?"

"Years."

"And your husband?"

"He left me soon after. I tried to find
my son, but I never . . ."

Owen rifled through his backpack
for the picture of him and his father
that he had carried with him. Could
his father have lived in the Lowlands
and somehow made it to the Highlands

with him? How? Why? Could the Dragon have known all along that Owen was a Wormling? Maybe he paid Owen's father to take Owen away and lie about his mother dying.

When the woman turned around, Owen handed her the picture, trembling. "Mother?" he said. "Is that your husband?"

"No," she said. "And my son would be only nine years old."

Owen fell into the chair, stunned and disappointed.

"You poor boy," Drushka said.

"My father told me my mother died the day I was born. He gave me this picture of you."

"How difficult this must be," Drushka said. "Let me explain. After the Dragon had burned the books, men came to our village with a strange box that flashed. They said they would give us exotic fabrics and thread as strong as rock if we simply wore the clothes they provided and stood in front of the flashing box."

"Then they must have put this book together."

"Yes," Drushka said, pointing. "That is my sister, and those are women from our village." She moved to a closet and returned with the very outfit she'd worn for the picture. "Older women would not do it. They feared the machine took something from you, shortened your life." She ran her hands over the length of the dress. "I wish I had not lived long enough to see my son disappear."

Watcher said, "The Wormling can help you find him."

Owen gave her a sharp look.

"I heard there was a Wormling in the land," Drushka said. "Is he near?"

Watcher nodded at Owen.

Drushka drew close. "But the Wormling is as tall as a tree and a great warrior."

"So I've heard," Owen said.

"He has killed demon flyers with one hand," Watcher said. "And he paves the way for the Son."

"I am the Wormling," Owen said. "Guardian of *The Book of the King*, though I'm currently failing at that. And a motherless son. I'm right back where I started."

"No," Watcher said. "You have learned this is not your mother. That is valuable."

"Great. I've eliminated one person from the Lowlands. I'll throw a party."

Watcher's mouth formed an O. "Well, you came to this world thinking your mother was dead. Now there is a chance you could find her."

Owen sat in silence, drinking in Watcher's thoughts.

"And if your father lied to you about me," Drushka said softly, "perhaps he is not your father at all."

"Unlikely," Owen said. "I look like him."

"That man in the picture?" Watcher said. "You don't look a *thing* like him."

"Sure I do. The mouth. The eyes. Our house cleaner even said I look like him. We even sound alike."

"What kind of a father would lie to his own child about the most precious thing in his life?" Drushka said.

Owen felt like an orphan, with questions for parents. Why would his father give him a book that led nowhere? Could his mother still be alive in his own world, the Highlands?

Owen resolved to find the King's Son and then go on a search of his own. For his past. He had to know where he belonged and to whom.

19

The Scar

The Dragon scratched the inside of his leg surreptitiously (which means he did not want anyone to know he was doing it). He had told no one about the scar left by the Wormling, nor had he described his encounter with the youngster, not even to his trusted (as much as a Dragon can trust anyone) aide, RHM.

When the aide entered with the Changeling, the Dragon quickly resumed his perch on his new golden throne. He had tried four throne makers before the drawings met his desires and the chair was carved. The first three throne makers—how shall we say it?—did not survive.

"The Changeling brings news, sire," RHM said. "He made contact with the Wormling."

"But you did not bring him back," the Dragon said, eyes turning red and boring a hole through the Changeling.

The Dragon's stare did not seem to bother the Changeling, who merely examined his own nails, chewed them, and disregarded the Dragon's belches of fire. "I performed the task you assigned, subdued the Watcher, and seduced the Wormling. I did not bring him back because I believe he is of more use to you where he is."

"You believe?" the Dragon roared. "It is not your job to *think*. It is your job to obey."

"True, Your Dragonhood, but let me tell you what happened—"

"What did he say when you told him what I would give?"

"He had questions, seemed interested at first. Then he shut himself off. Nothing I tried worked."

"Why didn't he kill you?" the Dragon said, fuming.

The Changeling turned into a female dragon, with long eyelashes and pearly teeth. "I suppose it was my charm and my—"

The Dragon grabbed the Changeling's neck and squeezed. "Do not trifle with me."

"Ckk . . . ahh . . . ackkkkk . . ." When the Dragon let go, the Changeling gasped. "I can still be of service to you, Your Rulerness. I have abilities I have not shown you."

"Why didn't you use them on the Wormling?"

"I wanted to get back here in one piece."

"Go on."

"I was *this* close, had him hanging over a cliff. Another second and he would have been a stain on the valley floor. But that cursed sword came flying up and—"

"What abilities?" the Dragon thundered. "What did you *do?*"

The Changeling turned into the Wormling, complete with backpack and sword.

The Dragon flinched, recalling how the sword in the expert hands of the Wormling had injured him.

"I made his mind race," the Changeling said. "I took the form of his father, a young girl from his school, and a younger friend. I read from his mind several passages from *The Book of the King*—quite inspiring, actually—and learned of this Scribe they search for."

The Dragon perked up. "Scribe?"

"In some mountain hamlet on the other side of the White Mountain."

"Yodom," RHM said. "That has to be where he's headed."

"Or already is," the Dragon said.

"He is obsessed with this Son business. If he can find him, the worlds will unite and blah, blah, blah, happily ever after, gag me."

"He will get nothing from the Scribe, correct?" RHM said.

"There is not much left of his brain, if that's what you're asking," the Dragon said. "Nothing but gibberish should come from him."

"It would be best," the Changeling said, "to trap your pesky foe in some unconventional way."

"Like what?"

"The Watcher is a problem, of course. She senses temperature changes and can detect the invisibles. Unless . . ."

"Unless what? Stop toying with me, man!"

"Unless beings attack from *under* the earth. She cannot sense those."

"The iskeks," RHM said. "A striking idea."

"I thought of that long ago," the Dragon said.

"Before the Wormling realizes what's happening," the Changeling said, "he will be entwined and immobilized. Then you can simply swoop down and toast him. Barbecued human. End of story."

"I shall not trouble myself with finishing him off," the Dragon intoned. He flicked a hand at RHM. "After I assign the iskeks, send a squadron of vaxors to confirm his death."

"Yes, sire."

The Dragon smiled wryly and scratched his leg again. "I've changed my mind about killing you, Changeling. You do have special abilities." He crawled off his throne and slithered

toward a black, globelike object in the corner. He belched fire
that made the orb glow.

> *"Foul one of the underworld, hear my cry.*
> *Rise to my bidding; the time is nigh.*
> *Slither and shake, the Wormling meet,*
> *Break through the ground beneath his feet."*

The orb grew clear, and a sand-colored path appeared.
Swirling like a tornado, the orb went dark except for two gray
eyes in the midst of the torrent.

What were these men like, Drushka?" Owen said. "The ones with the flashing box."

"Tall, with hooded garments, so I never saw their faces. Long, snakelike fingers. Repulsive. And the smell—the awful, smoky smell."

"Describe your son."

With a warm smile, she said, "He had the whitest hair—pure white. It was long and flowed down his back as smooth and silky as any woman's in the land. Deep blue eyes that could see right through you." She chuckled. "His ears stuck out like the wings of a bird. I wish I had a picture of him."

"What about your husband?"

Drushka's face fell. "I thought he was such a good man. And then he left. You don't know what that does to a person. Well, perhaps you do. . . ."

"What did he look like?"

She said he was of average height and had thinning hair with a bald spot and a large scar on his forehead. "He told me he had gotten the wound when a demon flyer tried to grab him, but I'm not sure that's true."

"Any idea where he might have gone?"

Drushka shrugged. "At first I thought he went to find our son. He seemed as upset as I was. The men he worked with at the stable said he was distraught. But one day he packed a bag and left. I never saw him or heard from him again."

When their questions were answered, including whether Yodom held a man known as the Scribe, Drushka filled a basket with pastries and breads for Owen and Watcher. "This will last you a few days." She put a hand on Owen's shoulder. "You have great strength of heart. I pray you find what you are looking for—and soon."

As Owen and Watcher walked to the middle of town, a horde of children followed. They found crude shops and a square where people gathered to talk, trade, and water their livestock near the stable—again a crude building with a distinct odor.

"So you're the one the children are so excited about," the

owner of the stable said, scowling. He sported a white beard, black teeth, and a patch over one eye. "Why don't you leave us in peace?"

"We mean no harm," Owen said.

"Like you meant no harm to the people of Shoam before they were washed away? Or the clan of Erol before the Dragon blasted them from their dwellings?"

"What?" Owen said.

"You heard me. They had lived in peace for how long before you came and *helped* them? We were told they have been destroyed. You flit around here in the open, begging for an attack, not caring what happens or who gets carried off when you leave."

Owen was shaken by the news of Erol's clan. He drew close to the man. "We'll be gone as soon as you answer a question about Drushka's husband. You worked with him?"

"Aye. Many years. More than you are now."

"Why did he leave?"

The man cocked his head. "Now there's a question I don't suppose has been asked more than a thousand times."

"You're hiding something," Watcher said. Her brows were furrowed, and the fur on her back stood up.

Owen spoke softly. "You can't fool her. She's a Watcher. Tell us what you know, what you haven't told Drushka."

The man let his iron clank in the fire and began rubbing a

horse down with a coarse brush. "He was upset about the boy. The night before he left, he told me his wife had met hooded figures who used a flashing box. He believed they took the boy. He didn't want her to know, fearing she would blame herself." The man turned and glared. "And if you tell her, so help me I'll burn you with a brand so hot—"

"Just tell me where he went looking."

"How would I know? I assumed he went to the White Mountain. But if you bring the wrath of the Dragon down on us, I'll personally cut out your heart."

Owen smiled. "When the battle between the Dragon and the Son begins, I want you at my side."

The old man sneered. "Don't count on it."

21

The Iskek

I hope I don't get that mean when I'm old," Watcher said as she and Owen left the town.

Children followed them to the edge of the forest, waving good-bye as they disappeared. The trees were so thick that Owen had to lead his horse.

"If we're not careful," Owen said, "we may never get that old."

"Why did he have to be so nasty?"

"Maybe deep down he's more sad than mad. Who knows what he's been through?"

"Yeah," Watcher said, giggling. "Maybe he was a Wormling as a child.

Sometimes you can be mean yourself. Maybe you're just sad. Or it could be all the jargid meat."

Owen's horse pulled away and walked off the path. "Come on, boy," Owen said. "Why can't horses talk here? Almost every other animal can."

Watcher turned to the horse and made a noise in her throat.

The horse whinnied, shook his head, and pawed at the ground.

"What did you say?" Owen said.

"I asked if he wanted us to name him."

"And . . . ?"

Watcher shrugged. "I don't understand horse, but he seems upset."

"All I need is a picky horse."

As Watcher led the way, Owen's thoughts turned to Erol and his family. Had they been wiped out by the Dragon, or were they on the run, searching for a safe place to live? Owen feared he had been responsible for their being attacked.

Watcher was still talking about mean people. ". . . Think of Mordecai and all he's been through, and you can understand why he's grouchy sometimes."

"Mm-hm."

"You're not listening to a word I'm saying!" Watcher said.

"Sure I am. 'Be more considerate of people even when they're unkind.' That's straight out of *The Book of the King*."

Watcher gasped and stopped, and the horse whinnied and reared, brushing the branches.

"What?" Owen said.

"I thought I saw something."

"You spooked the horse!"

Watcher rolled her eyes. "He's only sad," she muttered. "So, back to the book. It really says something about that?"

"Yes; a passage says that no matter what others do to us, we should treat them the way *we* want to be treat—"

"There!" Watcher pointed with her snout, and Owen glimpsed something moving along the path. The horse reared and broke away, galloping through the trees.

"Stupid horse," Owen growled. "It was probably just a mole or something. If you hadn't made such a fuss—"

"No!" Watcher yelled, starting off through the trees. "We have to leave this place!"

"But the village is this way."

"Hurry!" Watcher called.

Owen examined the path again, and it seemed to churn like a tornado, swirling storm clouds of dirt. He was entranced until Watcher raced back to him. "Follow! Now!"

But Owen couldn't pull away. The swirling on the path had spread to the tall grass and was more intense, so fast that Owen could hardly stand.

"Iskek!" Watcher shouted. "An iskek is under you! Run!"

Owen took a step, but it was like trying to walk on a shifting carnival ride. His feet sank and he jumped, trying to run, but he tumbled into the swirling dirt.

Watcher was screaming and the horse whinnying above the awful sound of stirring earth, but Owen was mesmerized by the scene below him.

Something grabbed Owen's ankles like a vise, and he cried out. As he began to sink, he yanked out his sword and punched it into the earth, trying to stab whatever was there. But each thrust seemed to hit nothing but soil.

Gray eyes appeared slowly before him in the dusty haze. Was this what Watcher called an iskek?

The pressure on his legs reached his kneecaps now, and he swung his sword toward the eyes. They darted and disappeared, and the hold on his legs became tighter, fiercer.

All Owen could think to do was recite from *The Book of the King*. " 'The King is my caretaker who gives all I need. He calms me and provides rest in the green field and points the way past the peaceful stream. He stirs my heart, strengthens me, and guides me to the right path. . . .' "

As the vise grip of the iskek slowly moved upward, Owen struggled for each word. " 'Even though I travel the valley of darkness, where my enemy waits to devour me, I am not afraid. The King is with me and comforts me. . . .' "

Was this how things would end? Had he come this far in

search of the Son only to be squeezed to death by an unseen enemy?

Owen dropped his sword and reached into the dirt, feeling the squirming, squeezing scales of something working its way up his body.

If this iskek reached his chest, it would squeeze the air from his lungs, and Owen knew his life would be over.

22

Watcher's Memory

Watcher stood helplessly on a knoll above and watched as the Wormling slowly sank. Bardig had told her that an iskek attack was the most horrible way to die. He had once climbed a tree and tried to grab the hand of a friend as he was pulled down by an iskek. Bardig's expression as he told the story was enough to make Watcher hope to never see such a sight.

She was vulnerable because she could sense things from above but not below. And because she was so light, an iskek could drag her under quickly. Bardig had warned her never to become complacent when walking in the Lowlands.

"One look into those lifeless, gray eyes, and you'll never make it," Bardig had said. "No one has ever survived an iskek attack."

Watcher raced back to the sinking Wormling, running around him, trying to avoid the whirling earth. She wished she had a rope to throw around the Wormling, but all she found was a rotting vine that snapped when she pulled it from a tree.

She used her teeth to pull on a sapling, but she couldn't wrench it from the ground. Watcher kicked at the roots, but the horse suddenly appeared and nudged her out of the way, grabbing the roots with his huge teeth and popping the sapling from the earth like a weed.

As Watcher dragged the sapling near the Wormling, she heard him reciting the beautiful words from *The Book of the King*. She had heard them many times on their journey, especially just before they went to sleep.

"Reach as far as you can!" she shouted.

The Wormling's breath was shallow. "No . . . stay back. . . . It will get you."

She pushed the sapling toward him, running it over the swirling ground, careful not to step into the vortex. "Take this!"

"I can't get my hands free!" he said, gasping.

"Then grab it with your mouth!"

The Wormling caught the sapling and tried to hang on, but he was left with a mouthful of leaves. "Can't . . . breathe!"

"Try again!"

He shook his head. "Find . . . the Son. . . . It's up to you. . . ."

"No!" Watcher yelled, and she spotted something on the Wormling's shirt. A white tail, and it seemed to be struggling to get free.

"Mucker!" Watcher whispered. "Wormling! Recite more of the book so Mucker will grow!"

The Wormling's eyes flashed, face red, eyes bulging. "Can't speak."

Watcher racked her brain, trying to remember some of what the Wormling had read and recited. Would Mucker grow if *she* recited the passages?

" 'Content is the person who . . . who does not listen to the advice of evil people . . . or even talk with them. But his pleasure comes from the King's wisdom and the words he has given.' "

The Wormling had sunk to his chest now.

Watcher couldn't see Mucker anymore, but she continued to call out the words. " 'Search diligently for the King's realm and his goodness, and you will be given everything you need. Don't worry about what will happen tomorrow. Tomorrow will take care of itself.' "

The Wormling took one last gasp as the sand reached his chin.

Watcher leaped into the swirling soil, shouting, " 'Ask the

King and he will provide; hunt and you will discover; knock on the door and the King will open it for you.' "

Watcher's forelegs were suddenly pulled under, and she called out, " 'As long as the King gives me breath, I will honor him and thank him!' "

Gray eyes pierced the sand, and Watcher continued, " 'Allow your heart the freedom it craves and then have the courage to follow it!' "

Something changed, and the grip of the iskek lessened.

Watcher struggled free and pulled herself out of the swirling soil. She called out more passages at the top of her lungs. She could barely see the hair of the Wormling now, but with a mighty push, he was up, gasping and coughing.

Watcher pushed the sapling toward him again, and the Wormling grabbed it, but a tentacle of the iskek's black body shot through the topsoil and encircled him.

Watcher grabbed the roots with her teeth and was then joined by the horse.

Just as the Wormling was being pulled back into the whirlpool, Mucker's wriggling tail shot out of the ground. With him came the iskek, almost making Watcher let go. Its eyes were gray pools of dread, its head the size of the horse, tentacles like an octopus's wrapping the Wormling again and again.

Mucker, grown to the size of a jargid by now, bared his fangs and sank them deep into the flesh of the monster.

When the iskek took one tentacle from the Wormling and wrapped it around Mucker, the Wormling pulled his sword from the ground with a zing and aimed for a spot between the iskek's eyes. The iskek shook the Wormling, and his sword nearly fell to the ground.

The beast rose from the earth, looming black and hideous over Watcher, the Wormling wrapped with two tentacles, Mucker with another, and supporting itself with several more. It looked like an upside-down tree to Watcher, with tentacles stretching out like limbs.

The Wormling hacked the tentacle holding Mucker, and he fell. He quickly sliced two more, sending the iskek teetering, and then the Wormling thrust the sword deep into the head of the monster.

Slowly, with a shudder and a whine, the iskek toppled. The Wormling chopped the tentacles holding him and dropped to the ground as the iskek crashed into the forest.

23

Aftermath

They walked from the scene in
silence, Owen leading the horse,
Watcher trembling.

Finally she said, "You know you're
the first ever to survive an iskek attack."

"I wouldn't have survived without
you."

The horse nudged Owen.

"All right, you helped too," he said.

Owen was finally able to smile. It
felt good to just breathe and not taste
sand and dirt. He had tried to hold his
breath when first dragged underground,
but the iskek squeezed around his chest
so hard that he'd lost feeling in his legs

and arms. When he went under, all he saw was blackness, an unending darkness.

Except . . .

He had seen a figure. A man? An angel? A demon? The being appeared to be dressed in white, with a short-cropped beard and salt-and-pepper hair. He looked unlike anyone Owen had ever seen, and yet he felt he knew him. The being bore a look of concern, but there was a sense of peace about him, as if everything would somehow be all right even if Owen was pulled into the depths. And when Owen shot back to the surface as if from a cannon, the man—or the vision—was gone.

Watcher's recital of *The Book of the King* had caused Mucker to grow, but now he was small enough to fit inside Owen's pocket again.

A few miles from the scene, Watcher said, "Do you want to stop? I see shelter above, and it's the heat of the day—"

"Keep moving," Owen said. "We should get to Yodom as quickly as we can."

Owen lamented losing Drushka's food in the iskek attack, but at sunset, which came frighteningly early on this side of the White Mountain, Watcher spotted an apple tree. The three ate until they were full. Owen enjoyed hearing the horse crunch the apples with his large teeth, and he was surprised when the steed sat by them as a dog would.

In the night, fog blocked the stars, and the path became

rocky. The horse became agitated, knocking a rock from the path. Owen noticed that it was several seconds before he heard it land.

"Let's stop here," Owen said.

"In the open?" Watcher said.

"Just until daybreak and the fog lifts." Owen took off his backpack and cleaned it out, then placed it on a rock and laid his head on it.

Watcher and the horse were asleep within minutes.

Owen closed his eyes, his father's voice echoing through the corridors of his mind. *"I did nothing to help you understand. I blocked you at every turn."*

Owen awoke suddenly in the morning, a chill rushing through him. The fog had lifted, and he sat up, peering at a sight he would never forget. Not five feet away lay a sheer drop into the valley. Talon marks marred the side of the rock wall. Across an expanse too wide to jump, the path continued.

Owen woke Watcher, who glanced at him knowingly. He had stopped them, had saved them from certain death.

"There must be another way to Yodom," Owen said.

Watcher winced. "Either up or down, unless we go all the way around the mountain, but that would take days."

The horse whinnied.

"The Dragon's minions will discover the iskek's body," Watcher said. "They'll figure out where we're going."

The horse blew his lips.

"Let them," Owen said, gathering his pack. "We can face anything now."

"Don't be too sure of yourself. A little fear sharpens the senses. We almost died back there."

The morning was clear, though a mist still hung on the mountain. They were high above the valley, but the mountain seemed to go on forever. They carefully made their way back, heading for the forest.

"Down there." Watcher pointed. "Another pathway that should take us to Yodom. And we don't have to enter the valley."

Owen was heartened, but the horse pawed at the earth and clucked.

"What's wrong with him?" Owen said.

"I told you; I don't understand horse beyond a few words."

By the time they reached the trailhead, the horse was lathered with sweat and his eyes darted. Watcher held up a hand.

Owen heard nothing. He moved out in front on the path, his sword clanging against a stone. To his left, the earth rose up, creating a narrow passage.

The horse stopped and nickered.

"Grab his reins," Owen said.

"No, wait. There's something up ahead."

"Invisibles?"

Watcher shook her head.

"All the more reason to hurry," Owen said. "We have to make it through this." He stepped forward, eyes on the end of the path that loomed like a tunnel.

Something moved into the light where the path curved down toward the valley—something large and upright, holding a stick or a weapon.

A horn blew and two figures appeared. Owen thought the musicians of Erol had found them, but these seemed bigger and menacing. One had horns on either side of his head and shook an object high in the air. Then a whoop rose like a cheering section at a football game, only lower in pitch, and more running figures poured into the opening.

"Vaxors!" Watcher said.

24

The Horn

Owen grabbed the hilt of his sword and fled up the path, Watcher and the horse in front of him, navigating the treacherous rocks. When they neared where they had slept, they stopped.

"We'll fight," Owen said, brandishing his sword in the sunlight.

The horse sniffed and shook his head.

"There are too many," Watcher said.

Owen looked above. "I can throw my sword and cause a rockslide to fill the path behind us."

"Nothing will keep the rocks from hitting us," Watcher said. "There's only one way. We jump the gap."

The horse whinnied and snorted.

"He says he can make it," Watcher said.

"I thought you didn't understand horse."

"Body language," she said. "His tail twitches when he agrees."

"We can't take the chance," Owen said.

Watcher moved toward the gang of vaxors racing at them. She stepped off 50 paces, turned, and began running, reaching full speed just as she passed Owen. She leaped at the edge of the chasm, a small rock falling into the hole in slow motion. Watcher soared over the chasm, stretching and, Owen thought, almost flying.

Owen's heart was in his mouth. If Watcher fell, she would never survive. She landed on the other side, stumbled, caught herself, and looked back, grinning.

The horse nudged Owen, and he turned to see human faces under all that vaxor hair. And they wore jargid skins on their feet. Their arms and chests were painted with black mud, and their skin looked rugged, like a crocodile's. The leaders of the group carried long knives, axes, and studded clubs. The biggest vaxor led the way, horns protruding, and he emitted a hoarse growl.

The horse moved behind Owen and stuck his head between Owen's knees. Owen slid down the animal's neck and grabbed the reins, galloping toward the vaxors.

"Death to the Wormling!" the leader shouted.

A cry from behind him reverberated off the walls. The vaxors were soon on them, gnashing their teeth and swinging their weapons. A huge vaxor with yellow eyes grabbed for the horse's tail. Owen pulled his sword and sent the vaxor veering off into a rock, banging his horns. The others keep coming, flailing their weapons.

"Go!" Watcher yelled from the other side of the chasm.

Owen's eyes grew wide as he and the horse neared the crevasse. Owen bent low, and as the horse leaped, he threw the sword into the path, where it stuck. Owen felt the power in the horse's neck muscles and closed his eyes as they went airborne.

Hundreds of feet above the valley floor, Owen soared with the horse's mane in his face, the wind in his ears. When they finally landed and the horse pulled up next to Watcher, Owen laughed and tumbled off and shoved his fist into the air.

Behind them, the horde of vaxors screamed and hurled clubs at them, most falling into the chasm. One vaxor with long, stringy hair pulled Owen's sword from the ground.

The leader grabbed it and held it high. "We have the Sword of the Wormling!" he shouted.

"Sword!" Owen called.

Immediately the sword shot from the creature's hand, and Owen caught it.

"Look!" Watcher said.

A chant rose among the vaxors as a tall gladiator ran the gauntlet, lifting off perfectly from the edge. "Death to the Wormling!" he yelled as he raised his club and sailed through the air, gray-brown hair swirling. He tucked his legs under, then stretched as far as he could. When he saw he wasn't going to make it, he dropped the club and reached for the other side. His knee struck with a sickening crunch, and the creature's face fell. He grabbed but came up empty, green fingernails scratching the dirt. Finally he tumbled into the chasm with a scream so bloodcurdling that Owen had to turn away.

"Unfair!" the leader of the horde shouted. "You killed a defenseless combatant!"

"I didn't touch him," Owen yelled.

A few vaxors tried scampering up the side wall, but the rocks were loose, and they, too, fell to their deaths.

The leader glared at Owen. "We'll get you, Wormling! I will have your sword and on it your head!"

The horde jeered as Owen rode away.

25

Names

Owen proposed the name Jumper
or Leaper for the lifesaving horse
as they hurried toward Yodom. He
didn't like Watcher's suggestions of
Bertwin, Redmund, or Gwilym. "Too
Lowlandish," he said.

"Humph," the horse said.

"Well, Wormling," Watcher said,
"yours tell only what the horse *does*.
You might as well call him Apple
Eater."

"Well, what do yours mean?"

"*Bertwin* means 'shining friend.'
See how his coat glistens? And he is
certainly your friend. *Redmund* means
'red-haired defender,' and—"

"His hair's not red."

"His mane is if you look at it from this side and the light shines just so."

"Humph," the horse said.

"*Gwilym* means 'resolute guardian,' " Watcher said, "and I think it fits best."

"Wait, what does *Wormling* mean?" Owen said. " 'The one who carries the worm'?"

"Oh, dear," Watcher said. "How awful not to know what your name means. *Wormling* means you are the keeper of the worm, yes, but it also carries the meaning of sacrifice—that you would lay down your life for your King if called to. Those who speak of you years from now will call you a champion of good."

"Words that should be reserved for the Son."

Watcher smiled. "Can you believe there will one day be a wedding our world will never forget?"

"*The Book of the King* describes it as a feast and a party," Owen said, "to which everyone will be invited."

"It sounds glorious."

"But we have to find the Son first," Owen said.

"Then what?"

"He finds the princess."

Watcher's eyes gleamed. "And the Son will unite both worlds, and there will be no more Dragon, no more sickness, disease, or death. . . ." Her voice trailed off.

Owen could tell she was becoming emotional, so he changed the subject. "In the Highlands, I was known as Owen." He spelled it for her and sounded out the letters. "I got teased a lot for it."

Watcher furrowed her brow. "I don't know why. It means 'young warrior.'"

"I mostly ran from fights."

"Well, when you return there, you will be much stronger—of heart and of muscle."

"What about you?" Owen said. "What does *Watcher* mean? 'Cantankerous, opinionated, talkative one who watches . . .'"

Watcher's eyes narrowed.

"'. . . and who has a very small sense of humor.'" He laughed and put his hands on her shoulders. "To me it means 'good-hearted friend; a constant companion with a fire in her heart for the King.'"

Watcher looked down. "It just means 'one who watches.'"

"No, it means so much more. It means 'one who follows diligently, ferociously, unceasingly, and wholeheartedly.'"

"Humph," the horse said.

"Wait," Owen said. "What does *Humphrey* mean?"

"'Lover of peace,' I believe."

"Are you a lover of peace?" Owen said to the horse.

The horse stared back at him until Owen pulled an apple

from his pocket and sliced it with his sword. "Perhaps you are a lover of a piece of apple?"

"Humph," the horse said, crunching the apple halves.

Watcher laughed. "Humphrey it is."

26

Yodom

The village of Yodom teetered at the base on the back side of the White Mountain. Shacks and buildings clung to the earth, and trees stood at weird angles, looking as if they could fall at any moment. Haggard people walked the trails, some carrying food for dinner, one hauling water up a treacherous hill. Children wearing threadbare clothing earnestly tossed rocks onto a massive pile.

Villagers seemed to eye Owen and his companions with suspicion. Perhaps they feared strange faces that could mean robbers or diseases that might wipe out the whole village.

Owen stopped a woman carrying

a load of wood and straw, her face deeply lined and her hair covered by a tightly-wrapped bandanna. She appeared to have three good teeth: one in the middle on top and two spaced unevenly on the bottom. She looked like the old woman with the poison apple in *Snow White*.

"Excuse me, ma'am," Owen said. "We're looking for someone known as the Scribe."

One gray eye clouded over; the other darted. Her voice was like fingernails on a blackboard. "Come to spy on us, have you?"

"Spies?" someone else said.

Word spread quickly, and children came running, chased by worried-looking mothers and men with pitchforks and long wooden spikes.

"The Dragon sent these three," the old woman said. "I can feel it."

"No," Owen said. "We come in the name of the King."

"He is a Wormling," Watcher yelled. "We seek the King's Son."

Three men menaced with their pitchforks. "If he is the Wormling," the leader said, "let him show us his magic." The man was brawny with bushy sideburns. "I've heard since I was a youngling that a Wormling could fly."

"I can't."

"I heard he can hover," another said. "Can you hover?"

"If I could, I wouldn't be walking, would I?"

The farmer sneered.

"Wait," the first said. "Can you make fire come from your armpits?"

Children drew closer, studying Owen. Others called for him to spin a web between trees, turn the sky green, and spit Wormling juice.

"I don't know where you heard these stories," Owen said, "but they're not true. I did come here from another world. I read from *The Book of the King* and—"

A gasp arose from the crowd, and the old woman pointed a crooked finger at him. "You can read?"

Owen nodded.

"Prove it!" She waved, and the farmers moved toward him.

Watcher growled and stepped in front of Owen, but he put out a hand. "It's all right. They're just confused."

The men took Owen to the center of town, where houses encircled a clearing. One of the men took Owen's sword and held it up to the sunlight.

"It's the Sword of the Wormling," Owen said.

"I can see what it is," the man said. "I just don't know how you got it. Did you kill the Wormling?"

"I *am* the Wormling. Why won't you listen?"

"Because the Wormling is ten feet tall with arms the size of tree trunks," the old woman said.

"Listen to him," Watcher said. "He *is* the Wormling. We have traveled—"

"Silence!" a farmer thundered. "Give him the scroll."

Another collective gasp. A young, round-faced girl handed a roll of parchment to Owen, her brown eyes melting his heart. All the children seemed frightened and unkempt.

"Read," the farmer said.

Owen opened the scroll, but it was in a different script. "I can't read this."

"Kill him!" the old woman said. "I told you they were spies!"

A roar rose from the crowd again, and the farmers moved toward Owen.

"Stop!" Owen said. "I can't read this, but I can read from *The Book of the King*. One portion says, 'Anyone who greets you on the path and offers so much as a cold drink of water will share in your reward. Kindness breeds more kindness.' "

"Where did you hear that?" the old woman said.

"He told you," Watcher said. "From *The Book of the King*."

"And where is this book now?"

Owen sighed. "The Dragon took it from me."

"I told you he was a spy!" the woman yelled. "He does the Dragon's bidding in exchange for this cursed book!"

"Listen to me!" Owen said. "For too long you've lived in fear of the Dragon, of demon flyers, of losing your families to the vaxors, who kill and steal and destroy. But the King wants you to live. He wants to bring you freedom and wholeness. He wants to bring you victory over the Dragon through his Son. I must find him, and I need the help of the Scribe."

The people stared at Owen, appearing surprised at the authority in his voice.

The old woman shuffled forward. "How do you know the Scribe lives here?"

Owen mentioned Mordecai, and the old woman glanced at the farmers as they moved away. "We esteem Mordecai here almost as much as the King," she said. "Did he tell you that he came through here and helped us many years ago?"

"No, but he did mention the Scribe lived here—"

"The Scribe is old and confused," a farmer said.

"The Dragon got to his mind," the old woman said.

Owen's heart fell. "Still, I would like to talk with him."

"He's telling the truth," the brown-eyed girl said. "I believe him."

The crowd grumbled, but soon everyone let the three pass.

Owen knelt and looked the girl in the eye. "*The Book of the King* says, 'You will enter the kingdom when you become like a small child, free of pride and willing to listen.' Thank you, little one."

27

The Scribe

Owen and the others followed the woman up a narrow path, where she pointed them toward the Scribe's home. "We protect him. He rarely comes out. Don't be surprised if you have trouble understanding him."

"What happened?" Watcher said.

She paused, her tongue passing over her three good teeth. "He was returned here one day by the demon flyers. A few of us helped nurse him to health and still keep an eye on him. Try not to upset him. He tends to throw things."

Owen thanked her and watched her amble down the mountain. They continued to where a shack sat in the branches of a tall tree. Owen climbed planks nailed into the trunk past limbs full of leaves and smelled something strange and wonderful. Someone was humming inside when Owen knocked tentatively.

The humming stopped, and a wizened old man stuck his head out and looked down at Watcher and Humphrey. "What a strange-looking animal," he said, squinting through thick, homemade glasses. Then he stared at Owen. "My son!"

28

Sock Soup

"Oh, you've come back to me," the Scribe said. "And just in time for dinner. Didn't you hear me calling? Have you been down to the water again? I told you not to go swimming."

The old man stuck out a wrinkled hand, and Owen grabbed it, pulling himself up and into the tree house.

The man's great, bushy eyebrows had grown so long that they hung over his eyes. His arms were spindly with loose skin hanging. He wore a tattered white T-shirt that exposed his bony shoulders. His head was turtlelike, with bug eyes and a sharp, poky mouth.

The man hugged him, and over his

shoulder Owen saw a thick, grayish stew bubbling and steaming over a fire.

In one corner lay a pile of sticks and firewood. In another, a pile of clothes heaped up as a bed. The rest of the place was strewn with trinkets and looked more like a child's room than a grown man's.

"Did you meet any friends at the water, Son?" the Scribe said.

Owen hesitated. "I don't mean to be rude, sir, but I'm not your son."

The man's face grew ashen, and he ran a hand through Owen's hair. "You didn't dive on a rock, did you? I've told you not to. It is quite shallow."

Owen gently took the man's hand. "Mr. Scribe, I've come here on the recommendation of a mutual friend—Mordecai. Do you remember him?"

The man's eyes glazed, as if he were looking to a faraway place. "Mordecai . . . Mordecai . . ." He snapped his fingers. "Was that the youngling inside the scrumhouse when you pushed it over?" He tilted his head back and laughed. "I'll never forget his face. My sides hurt just thinking about it."

The man took off his glasses and wiped his eyes. "Now please, let's eat before the soup gets cold."

Owen moved to the table. The stew seemed to be jargid meat mixed with fresh vegetables and boiled eggs. His stomach turned when the man stirred up an old sock from the bottom.

"I wish I could remember all your shenanigans," the Scribe said, dishing out a bowl for Owen.

"I'm not really hungry."

"Nonsense. You've been gone all day."

The sun was setting, and golden light glinting off the leaves gave Owen a warm but sad feeling. He was desperate to find the Son, but he couldn't help that this poor Scribe was a dead end.

Owen choked down a slice of jargid meat and smiled. "Good. You've outdone yourself tonight."

The man's eyes lit up. "I have, haven't I?" He laughed and clapped and stomped back to the pot.

With the man's back turned, Owen opened the door and poured out the soup, quickly turning back before the Scribe sat.

"Well, that was tasty, and I thank you," Owen said, rubbing his stomach. "But I have to be leaving."

"So soon?" the man said. "I thought you would stay and tell me stories like when little Mordecai reached into the jargid hole and pulled out a snake."

Owen smiled, pretending to remember. "We had good times, didn't we?"

"Yes, yes," the Scribe said, slurping his soup. "That's all

I have now—snatches of memories." His face scrunched in pain, and he put a fist against his forehead.

"It's all right. Remember the good times." Owen patted the old man and gave him a hug.

"Will you be back?" the Scribe said, his eyes cheerless as Owen opened the door. "Everything changes so quickly. There is nothing in this world I can count on."

Owen recited from *The Book of the King*: " 'The skies above and the earth below shall slip away, but the King's words will never slip away.' "

Owen climbed down to where Watcher was wiping her mouth with a foreleg. "The stew was good," she said, "but it had a strange aftertaste. What's it called?"

"You don't want to know."

"What did the Scribe say? Do you know where the Son is?"

"He's all mixed up. We should go."

"No clues? But we've come so far."

Dejected, Owen walked into the twilight, trying to find a place where he and his friends could sleep away from the threat of demon flyers and vaxors—like a cave or perhaps a hidden ravine. When he heard footsteps behind, tromping along the rock-strewn path, Owen pulled Watcher and Humphrey into a stand of trees.

However, Watcher's stomach growled, and the footsteps

slowed and stopped. Owen grabbed his sword, and when the branches parted, he thrust it near the face of the Scribe.

"You're not my son, are you?" the old man said. "You're the Wormling."

29

In Mind

Owen couldn't believe the change in the Scribe. His eyes were bright, and his face shone. Gone was the scattered look.

"When you said that, about the King's words, something snapped—a memory returned, and the jagged places of my mind seemed to come together. You must tell me more."

The Scribe took Owen and his companions to a secluded cave near his tree house. A strange odor made Owen think of a mix of jargid musk and oily gas from a filling station in the Highlands. The Scribe said it was runoff from inside the mountain.

He settled on a rock and began his

story. "I remember getting an engraved invitation to the castle from the King. It was such an honor I went a day early just to make sure." He put his hands on his knees. "My, it's wonderful remembering things. Well, the King asked me to show him my handwriting. He then dictated words that I wrote down carefully. After he studied my writing, he asked if I would be willing to come each day to work on a project."

"*The Book of the King,*" Watcher said.

"Yes, though I did not know its title then."

"What was the King like?" Watcher said.

"Mysterious. Kind. Wonderful. No matter what was going on in the kingdom, he always had a smile for me and a gentle touch. He would stand behind me, reciting. I simply wrote. He would often comment after a passage, something like, 'That will help them, don't you think?' And I would say, 'Yes, certainly,' but I didn't know who he was talking about."

The Scribe wrinkled his brow, and Owen worried the man's memory was fading again. But the Scribe looked up. "The King told me you would come. Isn't that something? He knew one day you and I would meet."

"How could he know that?" Watcher said.

"How could he know what to put in the book? Every story, every wise saying simply flowed through him to my pen."

"Did you meet the Queen?" Owen said.

"She would occasionally enter to talk with her husband. She was despondent."

"About losing her son," Owen said.

The Scribe nodded. "Of course. And it broke his heart as well, but something about him was always positive. He genuinely believed he would see his Son again."

Owen took a breath. "Do you have any idea where the Son is?"

"I gathered he was imprisoned. I have no idea where."

Owen bit his lip and turned away.

"Of course," the Scribe said. "That's why you're here. The Wormling searches for the Son. How I wish I could help you. I worked with the King every day for three years. I had to return to finish the missing chapter, but—"

"Chapter?" Owen said. "I heard there were chapters."

"There is a place in the book for an addition. Someone might think there are more than one because of the size, but there is only one."

"Tell me about it," Owen said.

"Just before the King disappeared, he asked me to come back and write it."

"What was it about?"

"That I cannot tell you. I did not write it in the usual way. I copied it from a special glass, and I carved it on a sheet of paper so hard it felt like metal."

"I don't understand," Watcher said. "Could you not read this chapter?"

"I'm sure someone could but not I," the Scribe said.

"What happened to it?" Owen said.

The Scribe winced and rubbed his temple. "That's . . . a good question. . . . I . . . you see, the Dragon did something to my mind. . . . I don't understand. . . ."

" 'Throw every worry and concern on the King,' " Owen said. " 'He cares for you and wants you to be free from the burden of your thoughts.' "

The Scribe's face broke into a wide smile. "Thank you. Those words wash over me like a mountain stream. What was the question again?"

"The missing chapter," Owen said.

"Yes, yes. The King presented the missing chapter to me for safekeeping. He wanted it kept separate from *The Book of the King* because . . ." A look came over him.

"Because?"

"He said one day the book would be stolen."

"He knew even that?" Owen said.

"Amazing," Watcher said.

Owen told the story of Mr. Page's coming to see him in the Highlands. The Scribe seemed astonished that Owen lived in a store filled with books.

"Where is this missing chapter?" Owen said.

The Scribe scratched his head. "I hid it. I know that. It was the one thing I was able to keep from the Dragon when he took me away. He did awful things. He poked around in my mind so that I could no longer think clearly. But by concentrating on the King's words, I was able to push that information far enough away that he could not discover it. But I pushed it so far that I can't remember."

"Think!" Watcher said.

The Scribe suggested they go back to his home. "It has to be there somewhere," he said.

Watcher's ears went up. "Someone is coming."

"Invisibles?" Owen said.

Watcher shook her head. "Human. And greatly concerned."

A light flickered outside, and someone carried a candle to the entrance of the cave. It was the old woman they had met earlier. She stared at the Scribe with frightened eyes. "I looked for you at your home!"

"I was helping these new friends."

She looked closer, turning his face with a hand.

"What?" he said.

"Where's the crazy man I knew? What's happened?"

"It's the most wonderful thing. I can remember. . . ." He paused, then looked deeply into the woman's eyes. "Rachel?"

They embraced and the woman wept. "Ever since the Dragon took him away, he's been unable to remember his family, his friends, any of us. For years I've brought him food and supplies, but it was too painful to stay. His mind was so clouded. But now . . ." She looked to Owen. "How did it happen? How did he regain his mind?"

Owen told her how simply reciting from *The Book of the King* had changed the man.

"I'm remembering things I haven't thought of for years," the Scribe said, "but I can't remember where I left the missing chapter."

The woman smiled and touched his face. "The important thing is that you've come back to me. My husband."

The two seemed to drink each other in with their eyes. The Scribe pulled away and looked wildly at Owen, then back at his wife. "No, I can't just put it out of my mind. The missing chapter is too important. The King gave it to me to safeguard from the Dragon—"

"And so you did, my dear," the woman said. "It is safe."

"You know where it is?" Owen said.

The woman nodded; then her face fell. "But I'm afraid you'll never get it back."

30

Rachel's Story

We worked as a team," Rachel said, stroking her husband's scant hair. "We lived in a cottage on the castle grounds, and I tended a portion of the King's gardens. They were the best years of our lives."

Owen said, "He mentioned a son."

The Scribe looked to his wife. "We had a son and two daughters, didn't we?"

She nodded.

"When the Dragon took me to find out what I knew and to erase my memory, he used—" At this the man broke down, his face in his hands.

Rachel whispered, choking back her own tears, "After his work on *The Book of the King*, we returned to our village. But by then darkness covered the land. The Dragon had heard about the book and wanted to know more. So he took my husband. . . ."

The Scribe wiped his eyes. "I wish I could show you what you're up against. Torture. Unspeakable pain. It's as if he were able to crawl into my mind and root around with his sharp talons."

"But he did not break you concerning the missing chapter," Rachel said.

"How could he? I did not know where it was. Only you did."

She nodded. "And when the evil one brought Patrick— our son—and said he would kill him unless my husband told him . . ."

"You couldn't give him the information," Owen said.

"Patrick was slain before his eyes," Rachel said, a tear hop-scotching down her wrinkled face.

Owen clenched his fists, his face flushed. If only he could have killed the Dragon in the castle instead of just slicing his leg.

"I vow justice for you and your son," Owen said.

"We can only hope."

"Now, about the missing chapter . . ."

Rachel said, "I put it where no one would think to look. Inside the White Mountain."

"Where prisoners are held?" Owen said.

She held up a hand. "Years ago there was no mining, and the place seemed remote, with many hiding places."

"Exactly where did you put it?" Owen said.

The hair on Watcher's back went up. "Something stirs outside." She ran to check.

Rachel lowered her voice, and Owen leaned forward, smelling her pungent breath. "Inside the White Mountain. It has a series of winding tunnels and passages deep inside. There was an entrance from this side, but the Dragon has sealed it off, and you can get in only through the pinnacle, which is treacherous and icy, even in the summer."

"How do the miners get in?"

"Flown in by the demon flyers."

"So I couldn't just climb it?"

"It would be a miracle if you survived the ascent. Humans lose their breath at that altitude. Ice forms on your eyelids and your lips crack and—"

"I understand," Owen said.

"Anyway," Rachel said, "even if you somehow made it to the caverns, you would have to find the exact place, somehow getting past the neodim who guard the entrance like sentries."

"Neodim?"

"Ask your Watcher about them sometime. Deadly is what they are."

"I defeated four demon vipers," Owen said.

"Very good," Rachel said, seeming impressed. She leaned closer. "Imagine a being five times as big as you with twice the deadly venom as those vipers. Better to just keep looking for the King's Son without that missing chapter. Besides, how would you read it?"

"Why did you take it to the White Mountain?" Owen said. "You could have hidden it anywhere in the village."

The woman looked around. "It seemed like a good idea at the time."

"You're not telling the truth," Owen said.

"Tell him, Rachel," the Scribe said, his face filled with questions. "Why *did* you choose the mountain?"

She sighed and her shoulders slumped. "A voice in the night said I should hide it there."

Chills ran down Owen's back. "A whisper?"

"Yes, but it was clear. I was to take the missing chapter to the Great Hall, and there were specific directions. But there were so many tunnels and passageways. In the inner recesses of the Great Hall, I found, just as the voice had said, a round design on the wall. As instructed, I buried the chapter directly underneath the design."

Watcher rushed back inside. "Invisible demon flyers are taking more prisoners to the White Mountain. And one is flying a scouting pattern. They may be leading the vaxors here."

"Vaxors?" the Scribe said. "It's been years since we've had to deal with their kind."

"Deal with them we must," Owen said. "Where is your meeting place in the village?"

Rachel told him and Owen stood. "One more thing. The design on the wall. What did it depict?"

"The Dragon," she said.

Someone sounded a bell, summoning men and boys of warring age. In the center of the village, a fire pit filled with wood blazed in the night, casting orange shadows. People gathered, whispering, tittering, rumors flying.

Watcher pulled the Wormling aside. "We should help these people and then use Mucker to tunnel inside the mountain."

"He hasn't healed from his battle with the iskek. I'm afraid we'd lose him forever, and someday I need to return to the Highlands."

"Soon it will be cold here," Watcher said. "I can't imagine how frigid it would be at the top. We should go as soon as the vaxors are vanquished."

The Wormling looked at her with kind eyes. "Watcher, you know how valuable you have been and that I would hate to go anywhere without you, but I need to travel alone."

"But the demon flyers. How will you elude what you can't see? And who knows what else lurks in those chambers?"

"Rachel says there are neodim."

Watcher closed her eyes, trying to shake the vision. As a youngling, she had strayed from the mountain and come upon a clear pool, where she saw her reflection for the first time. Trees swayed nearby, and a great thumping/crashing froze her in her tracks until she managed to back away from the water and retreat behind a rock.

She shook as a hideous being emerged, so ugly and menacing that she had to turn away. It snorted and gurgled and lapped at the water, then returned to the forest. Later her father told her that she had seen a neodim and she should never again stray from the mountain.

"What is this neodim?" the Wormling said.

Watcher shook her head. "I have seen only one and that at a distance, but even with your sword and all your training and cunning, I fear you won't get past one, let alone many."

The Wormling set his jaw and stared at Watcher. His eyes were like fire, but there was still a gentleness to them. "A portion of *The Book of the King* speaks to this: 'Do not trust in your strength or your speed, in your own wisdom or cunning, or in the number of your weapons. You must put your hope and trust in the King and his power, and he will guide you to the goal.' "

"What, are you to leave your sword and your most trusted companion here?"

"Watcher, your hooves would slip on the ice. I can't bear to think of you on some ledge, trying to hold on, freezing to death."

"I have a warmer coat than you."

"Stay with Humphrey and the villagers. If the Scribe loses his memory again, you could recite some of *The Book of the King*."

"And you?"

"I'll find the missing chapter, and then together we'll find the Son."

"What if you don't return?" As soon as she said this, she knew she had hurt the Wormling deeply. "I shouldn't have asked that, but I fear what might happen if you don't come back. Do I continue the search?"

"No matter what, we will see the face of the Son together. I promise."

A gaggle of voices came from the village center, and Owen hurried over with Watcher and Humphrey. Men spoke angrily to each other, shaking fists and raising sharpened sticks.

"You've heard the warning!" a tall man said, and the crowd quieted. Owen recognized this farmer, the brawny one with bushy sideburns. "A warring party of vaxors is headed our way. They may reach us by morning."

"It's *his* fault!" a skinny man said, pointing at Owen. "It was him and his spies that brought them to us."

The crowd turned. Sideburns moved away from the fire and stood in front of Owen. "What do you say to that?"

Owen stood tall. "I'm not a spy and neither are my friends. True, the vaxors may have followed us, but we will help you defeat them."

"He'll sabotage us from behind our own lines," someone yelled.

"Let's kill him now so we can focus on the vaxors!" another said.

"No, the vaxors are after these three. Let's give them up! The vaxors don't want us; they want them!"

The crowd cheered and moved toward Owen, but he did not raise his sword. Humphrey reared, and the front of the crowd backed away. A farmer threw a rope around Humphrey's neck and separated him from his friends. When a young man grabbed Watcher, she bit his arm.

"The vaxors do want us," Owen said, "but they won't stop there. They'll destroy your homes and the entire village. We must work together."

"We have a treaty with them," Sideburns said. "We have lived at peace with them."

"They are allied with the Dragon," Owen said. "They don't care about a treaty any more than the Dragon does."

The crowd became angrier and surrounded Owen. They took his sword and began to tie him, but someone shouted, "Stop!"

It was Rachel, along with the Scribe. "He and his friends came to warn you!"

"Spies!" Sideburns yelled.

"No! Look at my husband. He's back and thinking clearly because of the Wormling."

"What does this have to do with the vaxors?" another farmer said.

Rachel scurried forward, holding the Scribe's elbow. "The Wormling brings healing, not discord. He means you good and not evil. Listen to him and do what he says."

"It's true," the Scribe said, his voice shaky.

People recoiled, appearing surprised at his voice.

"The Wormling spoke healing to my soul. He can speak words of victory for your fight."

Sideburns stared at Owen. "Well?"

The men let go and Owen faced them. "We can help you defeat the enemy, but we must move quickly."

33

Daagn's Hopes

Daagn, leader of the vaxor horde, crouched at the top of the ridge and peered down with red eyes into the dark village of Yodom. His heart beat with a dull thud. His scout had sighted the horse the Wormling had used to jump the chasm. The enemy was near, and he had clear orders from the Dragon: Kill everyone. Do not leave man, woman, child, animal, or anything that has breath. The Dragon required only the body of the Wormling and his sword.

Soon the sun would cost the vaxor horde its element of surprise. Daagn was almost ready to signal the attack.

The massive, ugly creature had

narrowly escaped death when one of his men pushed him from behind. Daagn had frantically regained his balance, then casually pulled the man forward and tossed him into the abyss. He could not allow such an act, even if it might have been a mistake.

Grasping his ax, he whispered to his second-in-command, "Two waves, Velvel." (Be informed that the whisper of a vaxor is like your normal speaking voice. Their ears are recessed, and so much hair and wax and dirt are caked inside that they must nearly shout at each other to be heard.) "I'll lead the first from the left; you angle down, and we'll meet at the fire pit."

Velvel growled his obedience with excitement in his voice. "We will crush them, Commander." His nose was elongated, and he had more hair on his face than on his head. His given name had been Graadl, but as he took on the appearance of a wolf and ate ravenously, his parents had changed his name.

Daagn scanned the hillside once more with eyes that could detect movement in the darkness, unlike humans. But nothing moved. Even the smoke seemed to hang in the air, waiting.

It was not revenge that drove Daagn. The men who fell to their deaths had been weak or unlucky. He was glad to be rid of them. Neither was he spurred by some allegiance to the Dragon. He served the beast not out of devotion but rather from the fear of being devoured by that all-consuming fire. Obey or be killed. It was as simple as that.

What drove Daagn, however, was a desire for blood. A love of killing, of seeing opponents so scared for their lives that they were reduced to pleading. The begging made the victim that much more vulnerable. "Bury your ax deep enough to kill," he told his men as they practiced, "but not so deep that you silence their cries."

His forces, sporting war paint on their faces and arms, had not been home in years. They had traveled the countryside, laying waste to village after village. Some heard them coming and simply fled their homes and possessions. While that made a village easier to plunder, the joy of warfare and bloodshed was gone.

Daagn hoped this village would be different, perhaps as much sport as the first he had ransacked with his father years before. He had been put at the back of the line because of his age but had quickly moved through the ranks of fighters, wielding his ax. The vaxors struggled over walls and eluded boiling oil, and Daagn had arrived at the front in time to see his father crushed by a boulder dropped from the castle wall. Daagn had lingered, grasping his father's hand, fascinated by the blood that oozed from the man's mouth. Sadness and anger would come later, but at that moment he'd borne only a thirst for death to match the deadness of his own soul.

Now, crouching in the predawn darkness, Daagn licked cracked lips with a green tongue through pointed teeth. He ran a finger along the edge of his ax until a point of crimson beaded on the tip. He tasted it and smiled. The prospect of earth stained with blood beckoned.

Adjusting the animal skins on his back, he gave the signal.

Yodom was no unsuspecting village to the vaxor attack. The Wormling had come. The Wormling had warned them.

To Owen, the vaxors looked like animals, their fur pulled tightly across their backs, creeping up on some small, helpless creatures. Except the small, helpless creatures had been herded into the cave near the Scribe's home.

The vaxor leader crept directly past Owen's hidden spot as he led his troops north of the village. When he signaled his men, they grunted and salivated. At the same time, those below the village began their assault on the homes.

When the vaxors ripped off doors

and rushed inside, instead of cries and screams of frightened families, there came grunts and groans, coughing and sputtering from the marauders, and the splash of some liquid.

"Sir, there's no one here!"

"Same here, sir. Nothing inside except for this—" he coughed harshly—"liquid perched above the door."

A strong odor wafted over the village and carried up the hillside. The vaxors congregated in the middle of town, some wiping the smelly liquid from their faces, others staying upwind from them.

Suddenly Owen rose and called, "Sword!"

An orange glow shot from the fire and flew a few feet above the horde, spewing sparks on them. Those who had been doused with the liquid burst into flames and ran screaming through the camp. About a third of the army was on fire, with others racing away to keep from being burned.

Owen caught the sizzling sword with a hand wrapped in a jargid skin and stood at the top of the hill.

The vaxor leader whooped a war cry, and those not burning or running away started up the hill.

"You set a trap, Wormling!" the leader shouted. "But you have walked into ours."

The vaxors brandished their weapons and strained to get at Owen. But just as they drew within striking distance, he stepped back, raised his sword, and brought it down on a strand of rope tightly fastened to a log. The snap of the severed rope triggered a landslide of logs that barreled down the hill, followed by a cascade of rocks the children had gathered.

The vaxors turned and raced back down the hill, but they were no match for the logs and rocks that flooded over them. Other than a few lucky stragglers who had escaped the edges of the avalanche, only the vaxor commander remained upright. He had deftly danced to his right when the onslaught began. Now he raised his ax and charged up the hill.

On cue, the villagers —children bearing rocks, parents carrying pitchforks and spears—rose up as one from behind Owen and rushed the vaxor.

As if staring down a tidal wave, the commander slid to a stop and lowered his ax, then raised it quickly to block rocks and projectiles. He snarled and roared at the crowd.

When the volley subsided, he looked around. His troops lay dead or dying. His eyes blazed. "You will pay for this, Wormling!" He scampered down the ridge, over logs and boulders and dead comrades, disappearing into the golden horizon.

The villagers pulled bodies from the rubble and buried them—a grim task for even the strong of stomach. They found some vaxors alive, and Owen used his sword to try and heal them, but it did not work. He ordered the villagers to release the injured.

"Why don't we kill them?" Sideburns said. "If we let them go, we'll just have to fight them another time."

"*The Book of the King* instructs, 'Heap loads of kindness on your enemy so that in the end his heart might be changed.' "

"Surely you don't think these vaxors will ever serve the King."

Owen smiled. "The only vaxors without hope are those we buried. As long as there is breath, and as long as the King is in charge, everyone has hope. They're loyal to the Dragon because they believe they have no choice. The King's love will constrain them."

Sideburns stroked his chin and mumbled, "We heard rumors of a Changeling. A stark-raving madman regains his mind. Vaxors attack innocents. And you help us defeat a foe who would have easily wiped out the village. You *are* the Wormling."

"I am here to follow the King's orders. And my task is to find his Son so that all who wish to be free shall be."

Sideburns knelt before Owen, but Owen reached for him. "Do not bow to me; bow only to the King or his Son."

When all the villagers had gathered, Owen told them he was leaving. The very ones who had called him a spy and traitor now protested.

"The King's mission motivates me," Owen said. "But I will return. I'm leaving Watcher and Humphrey to protect you.

I can't promise more vaxors won't return, but I can tell you that they will never forget the village of Yodom."

It had been Watcher who suggested they use the fiery liquid from the cave, ignited by the Wormling's sword heated in the fire. She had observed the children playing with rocks and, with Humphrey's help, moved the logs into position.

Still, Watcher seemed glum as Owen led her to the home of the Scribe. When he told the man his intentions, the Scribe clawed through his old clothes and gave Owen a pair of shoes with sharpened spikes, along with a heavy coat and pants.

"These were my son's. I would be honored if you would wear them on your journey."

"I've prepared food and water for your climb," Rachel said. "Remember to drink plenty. The altitude will sap your strength."

Owen climbed down and bade farewell to Humphrey, and the horse nuzzled his shoulder.

Watcher had moved a few yards away and stood alone on the path. "I don't like that you're going alone," she whispered. "I hate saying good-bye."

"We're not saying good-bye." Owen reached inside his shirt pocket. "I want you to look after someone for me."

Mucker smiled through shattered teeth and rested on Watcher's back.

"I'm afraid it's too cold up there for him."

"I'll guard him with my life."

♦♦♦

Watcher sadly walked the Wormling to the edge of the snow pack, several hundred feet above the village, where a long stretch of ice lay before him. She looked up at the mountain and its twisting, blinding whiteness. Fog enshrouded the top.

"Be aware of a gust of hot air," Watcher said. "The demon flyers make slight squeaks. You can hide in the snow. And if it's a scythe flyer—"

The Wormling held up a hand. "I'll be fine."

Watcher stayed until the Wormling became a dot on the horizon, wiping a tear from her face.

35

Cold

Owen sank deep in the snow in places, his boots cracking ice in others. The first day he navigated the icefall—a long, shifting glacier valley—and by evening was exhausted. No way could he travel after dark, for the path, where there was one, proved narrow and treacherous.

He found a small indentation in the mountain and cut blocks of snow with his sword to fashion an igloo to block the wind. He carried no tent, but he had a supply of jargid skins to put beneath and over him.

As darkness descended, he settled in, eating some of the food Rachel had prepared. He drank water and refilled his carrier with snow so it would melt, then burrowed deep in the jargid skins.

As Owen drifted off, flashes of his life passed before his mind: his teacher Mrs. Rothem, the bookstore, his friend Constance. . . .

Owen sat up. Watcher had always reminded him of someone, and now it dawned on him. Constance. Her constant talking and analyzing and questioning. Even their voices sounded alike. He would have to tell Watcher when he returned.

If he returned.

Curled up here, his feet like blocks of ice, he wondered if he could accomplish this task. Just getting to the top of the mountain would be a first. And how would he elude the neodim?

Part of him couldn't wait to see one. Another part never wanted to see another malformed beast concocted by the Dragon.

A frigid wind invaded, and Owen buried his head beneath the skins, grateful that the curing process eliminated the horrible jargid odor. Again, as he drifted, his thoughts became a jumble of memories, finally alighting on a passage from *The Book of the King*.

> When I rise in the morning and go to sleep at night, I will think of you, O King. For you are great and powerful and majestic and full of splendor. The entire kingdom is yours. Truly you are lifted high above everything.

36

Words

Watcher stationed sentries on the outskirts of the village and made sure they had ram's horns to warn of an attack. She stared at the mountain, wondering how far the Wormling had climbed.

The day he left, a stiff wind had blown from the mountain, signaling the end of warm weather. All Watcher could think was, *If it's this cold down here, how cold is it up there?*

She played a rock game with the children, helping replace rocks that had plunged down the hillside. She let the flock shearer trim her face fur but, with winter coming, not any from her body.

Watcher also spent time at the Scribe's home—pacing at the base of the tree, listening to the laughter and soft voices above. When the Scribe spotted her, he insisted she make her way up on a contraption he had devised.

Moments later Watcher scanned the room, realizing that Rachel must have tidied up. The Wormling had described it as a mess.

The Scribe and Rachel asked Watcher question after question, going on about her life in the Valley of Shoam, her family, the attack of Dreadwart, and her travels with the Wormling. Rachel made dinner, and they talked long into the night. Watcher often found her mind drifting to the Wormling, wondering where he was on the mountain, whether he was warm, and if any demon flyers had passed.

Mucker slept deep in the fur on her back. She would leave him in the Scribe's home when she went outside so he could enjoy the warmth of the fire.

Suddenly the Scribe put a hand to his head and motioned for Rachel. "Another spell. It feels as if the Dragon is near and wants to drag me back to his lair."

Rachel made him lie down, but the man would not be comforted.

Watcher moved closer. "When your mind is clouded, remember this: 'Whatever is genuine, whatever is good, whatever is correct and clean, whatever your mind comes to rest on that is beautiful or brilliant—anything that is admirable or commendable—these are the things you should think about.' "

Like a man who hears beautiful music for the first time, the Scribe brightened and his eyes twinkled. Even Rachel seemed transformed by the words.

"How did you remember such a wonderful passage?" the Scribe said.

"The Wormling often read from *The Book of the King.* Some passages he repeated again and again."

"So, like the others, you do not read?" he said.

Watcher nodded. "The Wormling . . ." Each time she said his name it stabbed her heart. She missed him terribly and felt she was letting him down by staying behind. "He was teaching me, but it's been some time now. I suppose I'll never learn."

The Scribe stood and grabbed parchment and a quill. "Now, slowly repeat what you just told me."

Watcher was fascinated with the writing process. The letters looked different from the ones the Wormling wrote in the sand. These were polished—flowing and curvy—but when she recognized familiar letters, she clapped her front hooves.

Watcher studied carefully as she continued reciting, Mucker burrowing closer to her skin, gaining strength with each word.

37

Holed up

On the second day, Owen stepped carefully, digging his spikes in as far as he could, ascending the hazardous ledges. By the end of the day, his breathing labored in the thin air, and his fingers, toes, nose, and ears were numb. He looked for a safe place to sleep. Finding none, he kept climbing, the moon rising over his back, casting shadows on the ice.

When he reached a dense fog and the moon disappeared, he knew he was in trouble. He desperately needed rest. His arms and legs ached, and his stomach rumbled.

He recited from *The Book of the*

King, missing Mucker but knowing his little friend could have never survived this cold.

Close to midnight, Owen found a small ledge with two sticks jutting out. He wedged inside, draping jargid skins over his face. He ate a few bites of jargid jerky but found his water frozen. He licked the ice to get a few drops before falling asleep.

Owen awoke so cold that he couldn't feel his fingers. And when the wind whipped a jargid skin off his face and sent it whirling away, he looked into the sharp teeth of a storm that had come up during the night and bore down on him like a bull. Owen feared he could be sucked from his hiding place by the stinging snow and howling wind.

Owen was terrified by his loss of perspective. He had awakened to a world of white, a world without up or down. He didn't dare move.

Yet he still believed.

Believed the King had sent him here.

Believed the King had a plan.

Believed the Son was alive and would defeat the Dragon.

Believed the two worlds would be united.

And, most importantly, Owen believed that the small life he had led in the Highlands—the one cooped up with books in the back room of a musty old bookstore, afraid of the people around him and even his own shadow—had, in a strange way, prepared him for what he was about to face.

He believed there was something special about him and that the King not only recognized this but also celebrated it. Back at the bookstore, Owen had tried to simply blend in, to not bother anyone. Now he wanted more—not in a selfish way but in a good way, desiring that his life and the lives of those around him would be enhanced. He aspired to something more.

Owen reached with his tongue to catch snow and let it drip down his throat, but that only made him colder. Finally, around noon, he managed to open his backpack with stiff fingers and pull out another strip of jerky. The food warmed his stomach and made him feel like he could go on. But still the storm raged, and he had to stay put.

He knew from *The Book of the King* that no matter what was happening, no matter how bad the situation or the fight or the storm, a follower of the King could enjoy peace of heart and mind that could not be understood.

And so, as Owen lay shivering, lips chapped, body numb, he simply uttered, "Peace. Be still."

38

Progress

Something about the Scribe energized Watcher's desire to learn. He
was a good and patient teacher who
rewarded her with smiles and winks.

Still, she couldn't stop thinking of
the Wormling. Humphrey found her
after each of his romps with the children, but kind and gentle as he was,
not even he could replace her friend.

It had been three days since the
Wormling had left, and she could see
the storm raging on the mountain.
Could the Dragon have created it,
knowing the Wormling's mission?

Watcher closed her eyes. *Protect
him, O King, and bring him back. Not*

for my sake only nor for the sake of the people only but for the sake of your Son and your plan.

When she looked up, something swirled above her, finally coming to rest on a patch of snow. She loped to it, ice stinging her legs, and reached a jargid pelt, cut just so. Watcher gasped. It was one the Wormling had taken with him.

39

Power

Power surged through Owen, warming him like hot chocolate. The wind still howled, but the snowfall had mostly abated. And he could see again. A hint of blue worked its way through the fog as he crawled out of his jargid skins and stretched. He pulled himself up by grabbing the sticks behind him. On closer inspection, Owen realized these were not sticks but frozen arms. He brushed snow away and discovered a dead man's bald head.

Owen's mind flashed to the pictures of Drushka and her family. He put a hand on the man's head and grieved.

A gust of wind came from above, and a scream rang out. A man with long, flowing hair hurtled through the air as if borne by some invisible elevator. He seemed to disappear *into* the mountain, though Owen could see no opening.

He set out and focused on each step, every direction jagged and icy, and he could see all the way down to the valley. He secured his pack and chose a steep channel, a small stream cut into the ice. But with his first step, the ice broke with a sickening crack, and Owen plunged to his left, grabbing a chunk of rock jutting from the mountain. He dangled there, a block of ice attached to the spike on his left foot, his right foot stuck in the snow.

Owen tried swinging his leg up, but the ice block weighed it down. He tried to knock it off, but another crack made him wonder if the entire wall might fall away. His hand cramped, his right leg stiffened, and he had no place to anchor his left leg. Each breath became a wheezing gasp.

A wing flapped above, and an icy breeze blew through the channel, engulfing him in snow and mist. A squeak made him brace for sharp talons. Some choice. Be plucked from his perch by a demon flyer or plunge to his death.

Owen was running out of strength, his grip failing. And just when he thought there was nothing more to do but let go, a dark figure floated before him. It couldn't have been a demon flyer or he wouldn't have seen it. Was it some other concoction of the Dragon?

My mind is playing tricks.

Then Owen heard the voice—the same one that had encouraged him in the Highlands. "Free your foot of ice with the sword, Owen, and use it to move up the channel."

How long had it been since he had heard his real name? It both comforted and energized him. He hoped the figure, whoever it was, would be at the mouth of the cave to tell him which way to go if he made it.

Owen grabbed the sword and dislodged the block of ice, sending it skittering down the channel. He regained his balance and stutter-stepped like a lizard. The sword smoked as it touched the snow, and Owen gained momentum, finally pulling himself up to the entrance of the cave.

"Who *are* you?" Owen whispered. "Help me find the missing chapter."

But the strange visitor had disappeared as quickly as he had arrived.

40

Burden

The cavern branched into two paths, both strewn with human bones, and the ceiling dripped with something difficult to determine. The smell was like a mix of scrumhouses and dirty rags at a gas station.

Owen took the passage to the right, hoping it would lead him to the Great Hall. Rocks vibrated around him, and a deep rumbling swept through the mountain—an explosion? He talked himself out of running back out, and the cavern narrowed into a smaller opening that forked. Owen again stayed to the right.

A dim light flickered like a torch, but he realized the source was not actual flame but emitted by huge fireflies lolling on the cave walls.

The tunnel turned sharply to the right and angled down to where the earth grew softer. Something had left tracks an equal distance apart, and the oily-rags smell grew stronger.

Owen broke through what felt like a thick spiderweb and kept moving. A squeak sent him into the shadows, and when it became louder and more regular, he peeked out and spotted a beast slowly pulling a cart filled with jars. It looked like a donkey, but its head was more apelike with large eyes and teeth.

Owen stepped out of the shadows and said, *"Psst."*

The beast stopped. "Where did you come from?"

"Back there. I'm looking for the Great Hall."

The beast shook his head. "You are not going to live long, are you?"

"I hope to."

"You came through the web then. The neodim will find it has been breached." The eyes of the beast were as white as snow.

"You can't see, can you?"

"It's what they do to you when you enter the White Mountain. Take your sight."

"The humans too?"

The beast nodded. "All but the ones who fill the pots. They have to see."

"What's in the pots?"

"Liquid fire from below. It's for the Dragon's preparation for—" His ears shot up. "Under the cart. Quickly."

Owen scrambled under and held on as the cart began moving. They had gone only a few yards when something enormous rumbled through the tunnel, shaking the walls and causing a cascade of small rocks. Owen closed his eyes against the falling dirt.

The beast stopped and yelped as something savagely hit him. Owen got the idea that he had to move more quickly or face a more severe beating.

A horrible smell hit Owen, and his mouth dropped open as they passed the intruder's scaly feet, which appeared several times Owen's size, as Rachel had warned. Through the slats Owen saw glowing, green eyes and something that dripped on the cart and immediately burned through. Owen had to jerk his head to the side to avoid it.

"He'll be back looking for you as soon as he sees the web disturbed," the beast whispered. "Run ahead of me. The Great Hall is on the path that leads down."

"Thank you, my friend," Owen said. "What is your name?"

The beast kept walking. "We stopped using names the day we were brought here."

"Please," Owen said.

"Call me Burden. I bear the awful knowledge that what I bring will eventually destroy all life as I knew it. Who are you?"

"Call me Friend. I'm here to help you." He stretched his sword to the eyes of Burden, making the beast recoil. But when Owen spoke gently, Burden held still. There was a slight sizzling, and when Owen moved away, the white was gone and in its place were dark pupils.

"I don't believe it! I can see!"

"Don't let anyone know until the time is right," Owen said.

"And when will that be?"

"When the Day of the Wormling comes and when the Son returns to release the captives and give sight to the blind."

"But you just—"

A great roar split the air and rushed through, echoing off the walls. Seconds later it was met with the report of another roar, this one deeper and longer.

"The neodim?"

Burden shuddered. "No, just their helpers. Neodim cannot fit into these tunnels. You must hurry."

"Tell the others that the Day of the Wormling is at hand."

"What do you seek here?"

"The words to a book buried in the Great Hall."

"Words that change our destiny?"

"Yes."

Burden's eyes watered. "Why risk your life for ones whose lives are over?"

Owen placed his hand gently on Burden. "You are worth

much more than you can imagine. One day you will fight with us against the Dragon. One day you will see the deliverance promised by the King."

"Deliverance from this place?"

Owen drew closer. "Every captive will go free. And even the Dragon will one day kneel before the King."

Burden shook his head and groaned. "Here they come for you. You have given me sight just in time for me to see the death of our one ray of hope."

"I will not fail."

"Then hurry!"

Whoever or whatever the pursuer
was, Owen had no time to out-
run it, so back under the cart he dived,
facing up, holding on desperately.
Bouncing along, he felt his lips thaw-
ing. It was difficult not to bite at the
dead skin—one of his old habits—but
somehow with a new identity and a
mission of importance, he'd stopped
doing such things. He had stood up to
the Dragon and his evil companions
and had even spoken persuasively
to villagers who wanted him dead.
And he had done it with authority
bestowed by the King.

Burden whispered desperately as he
hurried along, "We'll come to a larger

tunnel soon. If the neodim don't stop us, I'll take you to the Great Hall."

Two other beings passed, smacking Burden almost as if only for sport.

"I would give anything to defeat those brutes and destroy this mountain," he said.

"Patience, Burden," Owen said. "It will be destroyed but not now."

Burden stopped. "You aren't going to release us?"

"Keep moving," Owen whispered. "First I have to find what I'm looking for. Where are the prisoners?"

"Deeper, harvesting what's in the jars, and I must be careful. Even a spark reaching the liquid would leave nothing to search for."

Ahead of them, shadows moved in front of a flickering lightning bug.

"Have there been explosions?"

"Small ones. But still they push us. Now be quiet. We are coming to one of the main caverns."

The cart bounced, and through the spaces in the slats, Owen noticed bearded workers in sweat-stained shirts digging with long metal picks. They looked worn to exhaustion.

A bug-eyed beast with a whip lashed Burden's back, seemingly for no other reason than to keep him moving. The newly sighted creature cried out, and it was all Owen could do not to spring out and use his sword.

"'Bout time you got here," Bug Eye growled. "Any sign of an intruder?"

"Intruder? Who'd be foolish enough to come here and risk being put to work? Just another laborer for you."

Bug Eye snickered and lashed Burden again. "Keep moving."

Owen soon realized that these haggard, sweaty men were digging another tunnel. They carefully took the jars from the cart and placed them along the digging line.

"Move along!" the taskmaster yelled, brandishing his whip.

Burden ambled away, heading for a large opening.

When they were safely away, Burden said, "Many of those men will die in the blast. Some are so sick of working here that they throw themselves into the explosions."

The cart clacked down the wider tunnel. "Can the neodim fit here?" Owen asked.

"Oh yes, and they have been alerted to an intruder by now. They're no doubt following your path."

A high-pitched alarm that sounded like a ram's horn ripped through the tunnel, followed by a terrific explosion. Soil and rocks clattered down, and choking, blinding dust rolled through.

Owen covered his face with his shirt and fought to breathe.

Watcher heard thunder but didn't see clouds, and she couldn't shake the feeling that something had gone wrong with the Wormling's mission.

She didn't sleep well because of her dream of the Dragon chasing her through the forest, fire shooting from his mouth. Another was of vaxors rising from their graves and attacking villagers, gnashing their teeth as they chased children.

The worst was of a procession trudging down the White Mountain, slipping and sliding through the snow. They carried a wooden pallet and on it a body hidden under a cloth shroud.

Watcher pulled it off with her teeth, revealing the dirty face of the dead Wormling.

Then a horn sounded, a warning that blew from the east and roused Watcher from her sleep.

Villagers passed Watcher as she hurried into town, pushing children, trying to get them to safety.

"Vaxors!" someone said. "Returning to kill us!"

A man pointed at Watcher. "You and that Wormling got us into this. Where is he when we need him?"

Watcher kept running, and Humphrey joined her, nudging her as they galloped along.

They were met by a runner, a young boy who shouted, "They're coming quickly, and they have weapons! They've gone into a ravine below us."

"How many?" Watcher said.

"One hundred. Maybe two. I can't tell because they're spread into several groups and—" His voice caught and he whispered, "The first group is coming over the ridge."

43

Hot Breath

To know your enemy is the first
step of a warrior," Mordecai had
taught Owen, but Owen was certain he
didn't want to get to know the neodim.

Burden pulled the cart down long,
spiraling passages, some so steep that
he simply let the wagon push him.
"Bump coming," he called.

Owen was nearly jostled from
underneath. "Thanks for the warning."

The path flattened, and they
entered a cavernous room with a sheer
drop on the edge. Water cascaded from
a hole in the opposite wall and pooled
at the bottom.

"A little farther now," Burden said.

Owen leaned from the precarious

edge of the path, a feeling of power sweeping through him just knowing he still had the Sword of the Wormling.

Darkness blanketed them as they entered another tunnel. "Very steep here—you may want to walk the rest of the way."

Owen let go, and the cart rolled past him. He felt his way along the wall, noticing that Burden's groans and grunts had turned into panting.

The farther down they went, the cooler and mustier the air became. Owen became preoccupied with the smell of the liquid that coursed down the walls—it smelled like gasoline—and suddenly there was no sound of his new friend or the cart.

"Burden?" Owen whispered. He felt along the wall with one hand and used his sword to test the path ahead. He saw no more with his eyes open than closed.

A rotting, putrid smell, like the garbage can behind the Blackstone Tavern or a dead animal, hit Owen's nostrils.

How he wished that was all it was when a snorting growl blew hot breath on the back of his neck.

44

Company

Watcher moved under the tree of a sentry, who reported from above. "They're just beyond the knoll," he whispered. "Coming this way."

Watcher hid in the bushes. If these were warriors like the others, a few untrained villagers would be no match for them.

She peered out at the invaders and saw spears and wooden pitchforks, along with bare human feet. No red eyes or furry backs or sharpened metal. These were villagers, much like the people in Yodom.

"Hello there," Watcher said, stepping out.

The men recoiled, taking cover, one putting an arrow into his bow.

"Wait!" someone said. "It's her!"

The man let the string go limp and put down his bow. Others ventured out.

The leader, a large man with pudgy fingers, squinted at Watcher. "Are you the Watcher of the Wormling?"

She nodded. "Who are you?"

The man knelt and bowed his head. "Treyhol, guard of the three valley towns at the river. News of your fight against the vaxors reached us. We want to join your warring party."

"We have no warring party," Watcher said. "How many are in your group?"

"Four companies of fifty. We do not have advanced weapons, but we are ready to join you."

"How did you hear?" Watcher said.

"News of the Wormling is spreading through the land like wildfire. Where is he?"

"On a mission, but—"

"Did you hear that, men?" Treyhol called. "He prepares to battle the Dragon."

The men whooped and yelled, and their cries spread to the companies behind them.

"You don't understand," Watcher said. "The Wormling does not prepare for war; he is looking for—"

"If it's all right," Treyhol said, "we'd like to stay in the village until he returns for battle."

"You can stay, but the Wormling is not ready—"

"Forward!" the leader yelled.

45

Neodim

Owen froze.

Demon flyer? Neodim? One of the bug-eyed minions of the Dragon?

He drew his sword and raked it against the wet wall, the weapon hissing as it met the moisture. Owen lit out as fast as he could go, racing through the tunnel and away from whatever was behind him. At a sharp turn, he fell, and the sword stuck in the wall. He called for it and caught it in the dark, scrambling to his feet as he was chased by what sounded like the freight train that rumbled through his town in the Highlands. The tunnel vibrated, the walls shook, and soil and rocks fell.

Owen saw a pinprick of light ahead and heard squeaky wheels. The point of light grew as Owen hurtled closer and the tunnel flattened. Burden ambled along.

"Watch out!" Owen yelled as he shot past the cart.

"You were wondering what a neodim looked like," Burden said. "You're about to find out."

Burden pulled his cart to the side, the rumbling ceased, and Owen backed up, his sword at his side.

"Stop right there," Burden whispered.

Owen found himself on the very edge of a precipice. The massive floor of the cavern below stretched to rocks on either side that vaulted like the pipes of a huge organ, majestic and beautiful and somehow full of light.

"Stay where you are, intruder," something said with a voice so low it shook Owen's clothes.

With his back still turned, Owen said, "I thought neodim were too stupid to speak."

"Turn and face me. I want to see you when you die."

Owen turned to find the entire opening of the tunnel blocked by the massive creature. His legs wobbled, and he stuck his sword in the ground to steady himself.

"First time seeing a neodim?" the mocking creature said.

"Yes, and I hope it will be the last."

"Mm-hm. I assure you, it will be." The neodim squatted, then rose to full height, as if limbering up. It towered over

Owen. The huge, ugly, black eyes were set on either side of a wolflike head with a large snout and long incisors. Its long hairy arms led to claws as thick and sharp as the Dragon's talons.

The neodim stood on its hind legs like a bear, tail encrusted with dirt and clay. "Think you're fast enough to use your sword?"

"I may be small, but I serve the King."

"I serve the coming king," the neodim growled. "And soon this Great Hall will launch his sovereign rule."

"Why here?"

"So many questions," the neodim said. "And so little time for answers."

"It's just like the Dragon to use this wretched place."

A howl pierced the chamber, and another neodim emerged from a tunnel in the floor below and glared up at Owen.

"The Dragon will begin the cleansing right here. The mountain will open, and he will descend, and with a blast of his breath, he will ignite the consuming fire."

Owen smirked. "Sounds like it will consume you as well. You and your brother down there."

Three more neodim appeared below, waiting, prowling, studying Owen.

Owen caught a glance from Burden. The animal moved slightly, revealing a smaller tunnel, one the neodim was too big to enter. But if Owen escaped, what would the neodim do to Burden?

"Throw him down!" a neodim called. The four circled and howled, grinding their teeth.

The neodim near Owen opened its mouth, and a red tongue protruded, the monster's lips foaming white. The Slimesees had given him the same look before Owen sent it reeling.

" 'Listen to the King and obey him,' " Owen said, " 'for this is the way of wisdom.' "

The neodim lunged at Owen, who raised his sword. The neodim roared and swatted it out of Owen's hand, and it clanged down the side of the rock wall.

"Sword!" Owen yelled.

It returned as the neodim lunged again. Owen ducked and rolled, his foot slipping over the edge. As the monster charged, muscles rippling, Owen drove the sword into its shoulder, and blood gushed.

Owen tiptoed along the edge of the chasm. The other neodim jumped and roared below. One wrong step and he'd fall into their clutches. The wounded neodim was on him quickly, making Owen teeter on the edge. The only way back was blocked by the neodim.

The beast spread its claws and stood at full height. "You will regret coming here, Wormling!"

Owen swung his sword over his head with both hands and threw it at the heart of the beast, but the neodim dodged it, the weapon clanking off the rock wall behind him.

With a sudden thump from behind, courtesy of Burden, the beast howled and lurched toward Owen, out of control. Owen dodged as the neodim stuck its claws into the rock, desperately trying to regain its balance. Owen quickly nudged it over the edge, and with a crash and shudder of earth, it landed and lay motionless.

"Quickly, through here," Burden said. "The others are ascending."

Watcher didn't know which was worse: a horde of vaxors descending on the camp or all the amateur fighters joining them from the surrounding valleys. Who would feed them and where they would sleep?

When a hunting party returned with jargid and made cooking fires in makeshift pits, the villagers complained of the smoke and noise.

Concerned parents cast scornful eyes at these fighters—many of whom were young and meant no harm, but their mere presence seemed threatening.

Soon the blame fell on the Wormling. He was the one, so the

fighters believed, who had single-handedly killed the vaxors and brought down countless demon and scythe flyers. Watcher tried to explain, but the anger of the villagers would not be quelled. How could she and the Wormling have known that their search for the Son would stir up so many villagers?

"This was your plan all along," Sideburns said to Watcher. "After all those years waiting and watching, you desire the credit!"

"I desire only to serve the Wormling, thereby serving the King."

Finally the Scribe hobbled before the group. Watcher could tell the villagers revered him, although it was clear that some still found it hard to believe he had regained his mind. His words fell over them like soft rain. "These friends, the fighters, have come to keep a vigil for the Wormling. The least we can do is welcome them and thank them. If the vaxors return, they will be sorry."

The Scribe turned to the army. "And you will be considerate of our customs and our people. We will share food and provisions. You will wash daily and not influence our children.

"Finally, I say, whoever fights our enemy is my friend. And whoever means to slay the Dragon is my brother."

47

The Great Hall

"Thank you for what you did, Burden," Owen said when they stopped to rest. "Your push sent him over the cliff. I just helped."

Burden's breath was heavy. "We must keep moving. The others are on their way."

"Where does this lead?"

"To the Great Hall. Isn't that where you wanted to go?"

"Yes, but those four neodim—"

"They'll look for you in the tunnels. And there are more than four, you know. Soon the whole company will be here."

Horns blew through the underground, alerting others of the intruder.

Neodim shouted their high-pitched howls that echoed off the walls.

"Let's start in the workrooms," Owen said. "Some there may be able to fight with us."

Burden shook his head. "If you can free them."

Seven workrooms held prisoners who toiled while chained together in a long row. They worked in tattered clothes, faces and hands stained with dirt. They filled pitchers with the liquid flowing out of the mountain and transferred them to carts. When the liquid stopped flowing, they used picks and shovels to open the rock until it flowed again.

Owen scanned the row of workers, then moved to the next room. When he and Burden reached the third room, he spotted the man he was looking for.

Connor sat near the end of the row, his jaw set, pouring liquid and stretching at the chains. Connor's ankles were raw and bleeding, his back bloody, and his face bruised.

Owen slipped up behind the beast watching the workers, cracking a whip and poking a long, spearlike weapon that shocked them. Using the hilt of his sword, Owen conked it on the head so hard that it fell forward, bouncing on the ground.

The men turned and cheered, but Owen quieted them.

"Come to gloat, Wormling?" Connor growled.

"The Wormling?" another said, falling to his knees and clasping his hands. "Please, sir. My wife is also here—"

"This is not a rescue mission," Owen said. "At least not yet." He turned to Connor. "There is something in the Great Hall I need, so we must create a diversion."

"And then you'll leave us to rot?" Connor said. "It figures."

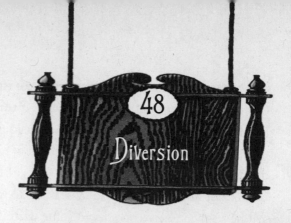

Though Connor was a newcomer, along with Gunnar and others of his fighters, he had quickly earned the respect of the other prisoner workers. It had taken several beasts to secure Connor, and he'd had to be knocked unconscious.

As one might suspect, Connor had been cooking up his own escape plan, which included using the explosive liquid to wipe out the enemy. If a few prisoners were also killed, Connor could live with that. And if things really went badly, he could simply blow up the whole mountain. The prisoners would die too, but a major battlefront of the Dragon would be destroyed.

Those plans changed with the arrival of the Wormling. Connor was surprised the kid had made it this far. That he had killed a neodim was an impressive accomplishment but also a headache. The rest would become like bees around a disturbed hive.

Connor did not expect the Wormling to understand this. All he seemed to care about was some writing hidden in the Great Hall, as if words on a page could change anything. Connor knew the only way to do that was to defeat the Dragon.

Once the captives in the workroom were freed, Connor took the keys. "I have to find my wife."

"You agreed to help," the Wormling said, fire in his eyes.

"Do you know what will happen if you find that precious scroll? The neodim will crush you. And if you somehow escape, they will descend on us and make us pay for your victory."

"I do not want that."

"And yet you cannot deny it," Connor said. "You know these beasts have no mercy."

"But they want you alive so you can work."

"They will find others, ones they can easily pick from the valley." Connor seethed. "Your presence seals our fate—unless you allow us to fight. First we release all the workers."

"No, we must find—"

"If we don't release them now, we'll never have another chance."

The Wormling pulled away to confer with the beast of burden who had accompanied him. After a few moments he returned. "Give your most trusted aide the keys and half the men to release the others. You and the rest come with me."

"Agreed," Connor said.

⋙

Owen did not like negotiating when he should have been looking for the scroll, but he also did not want to leave dead people behind. His search had become a rescue whether he liked it or not, but he was content to leave that in other people's hands.

Connor and some others followed him and Burden through the snaking corridor that led to the Great Hall. Owen left them and crawled down a narrow entrance to find three neo-dim standing watch, talking among themselves.

"I hope they don't kill him before I get a piece of him," one said.

"You'd better hope they kill him before he comes down here," another said. "He may be small, but you see what he did to our comrade."

"He was our best. He must have made a mistake—left himself open. . . ."

"You've bought into the notion that there is power only in the one we serve," the first said. "I also sense great strength in this Wormling. It is up to us to stop him."

Owen crawled back, bolstered—a strange place to get encouragement. He and the others were ready to attack when a runner—a young boy—flashed through the tunnel.

"They need your help," he said, breathless. "A neodim has them pinned."

Owen grabbed Connor's arm. "We had an agreement."

"These are my people," Connor said.

"Your wife," the boy said. "She's hurt."

49

Connor's Wife

Owen followed Connor and the others and entered the second work area to find that half of the line of men and women had escaped. The others were bunched on the other side, where a neodim bent over a terrified woman, teeth bared, ready to pounce.

"Dreyanna!" Connor shouted, rushing the monster.

Its razor-sharp talons were at the woman's neck. One move and the animal could take her life.

Owen drew his sword and yelled at Connor to stop. "Anger is not our best ally," he whispered. "Control your rage to defeat your enemy."

"Harm one hair on her head,"

Connor spat at the neodim, "and you will face the same fate as your dead brother!"

"Stay back, Connor!" Dreyanna called out. "It's over for me."

Connor signaled Owen as he moved to his right, near the pool of liquid. Owen took the cue and moved left.

"The human wants his wife back?" the neodim said. "In how many pieces?"

Connor, now next to the pool of liquid, held up a hand. "You don't have to die. Leave her."

"*You* offer *me* a reprieve?" The monster shook with laughter.

"No one has to know this escape was your fault. And when the Wormling slays the rest of the neodim, he will allow you—"

"That runt killed him?" the neodim said, turning. But Owen was now behind it. "Where is he?"

Owen swung quickly and sliced the neodim's arm holding Dreyanna. She fell as the neodim howled.

"Temper, temper," Owen singsonged, moving away. "We gave you a chance to surrender—"

The beast called for backup as Connor gathered up Dreyanna and ran for a tunnel. The neodim swung its tail and sent them both to the ground, but Owen was just as quick, lunging and slicing three of the monster's talons from its remaining paw.

With great speed and force, the neodim sprang at Owen, jaws open, teeth dripping, and Owen thought he might have miscalculated. He jumped away just in time but felt the wind from the beast's arm pass his face. Owen thrust his sword, piercing the neodim's heart. Its arm went limp.

"The neodim are coming," Burden said.

"Take the keys and release the others," Owen said. He rushed to Connor and Dreyanna, still dazed on the floor. He helped them to their feet. "Hurry!"

50

Trapped

By the time Owen made it to the other workrooms, the neodim had blocked the tunnels.

A pitter-pat akin to soft rain on palm leaves echoed through the workroom. Connor picked up the shocking stick near the neodim's body.

"Here come the movals," Burden groaned.

What now? "Do they have talons? venom?"

"Just ugly creatures no one can stand," Connor said.

The movals proved to be a sightless, faceless race used to herd humans. They poured through the openings like water.

People backed away, repulsed by their smell and appearance.

Owen stepped back and nearly turned over one of the pitchers of combustible liquid. He tossed some on the front of the line, and the movals screeched and retreated. Others flowed forward, and Owen doused them.

"Careful," Connor said. "You'll blow the whole mountain."

"Great idea," Owen said. He moved toward the main tunnel leading to the Great Hall, spreading the liquid and pouring it on his sword, creating a black plume.

"Wait—you want to blow this whole thing and kill us all?"

"No, but I want the neodim and the movals to think I'm willing to. Follow me."

The movals retreated into the Great Hall, to the chagrin of the neodim. Their company had swelled and seemed just as repulsed as the humans. When the neodim saw Owen and the others carrying pitchers, they advanced.

"Stop," Owen said. "These are full and we'll use them."

"We do not negotiate with prisoners," the largest neodim said. "Seize them!"

Owen splashed the pitcher on three neodim. They wiped at the liquid, looked back, then kept coming. Owen scraped his sword on the stone, sending sparks onto the three, making them burst into flames as they screamed and rolled.

Several other neodim threw dust and sand on them to put out the fire.

"We know the Dragon's plans," Owen said. "He will not be able to use this mountain and its resources if it no longer exists."

"Meaning?"

"Mountain goes *kaboom* and your lives are over. So is the Dragon's plan."

"You would kill yourselves to thwart the Dragon?"

"For the good of the land and the people we love."

"The alternative?"

"Release us. Let us go back to our families and live in peace."

"We know of you," the neodim sneered. "You have no family here."

Owen lifted his sword over his pitcher. "All the more reason to end this now and send you howling back to where you belong."

"Wait," the neodim said. "Let our council meet."

"Quickly," Owen said. "And leave the hall."

Others rose behind him, glaring, but when another spark flew from Owen's sword, they recoiled.

"Leave us," Owen said.

As Owen had hoped, the neodim retreated through the largest tunnel, grumbling.

Finally alone, Owen recalled Rachel's words and searched the front of the hall. He plunged his sword into the crumbling earth until he hit something solid, then dug with his hands and uncovered a leather satchel.

"Excuse the intrusion," Connor said sarcastically, "but do you have a plan? Or are you just on a scavenger hunt?"

Owen opened the satchel and pulled out a long piece of metal. Though dirty, it looked in perfect condition. He slipped it back inside and put the satchel in his backpack. "All right, are you ready to fight?"

"We have no weapons save your sword and this shocking stick," Connor said.

"True. But we have the greatest weapon of all."

"The exploding liquid?"

"The King's blessing. It is his wisdom we must rely on now."

"And what would the King suggest in an instance like this?"

Owen turned to Burden. "The lowest point of the tunnels. Where would that be?"

Burden nodded. "The last chamber where your people are held."

Owen wished he knew exactly how far underground they were or that he had Mucker with him to help. He moved toward Burden and plucked a tuft from his long tail.

"Ow!"

Owen examined the hairs. "It just might work. Then again, we could all be killed."

"What are you muttering about?" Connor said.

"I'll explain on the way."

The entire company moved to the last workroom, which had been sealed off by a huge boulder. Owen's cries were answered by the people. "They've left us alone—we can't breathe!"

"Stand back from the opening!" Owen said.

With Burden's help, Owen and the others moved the boulder enough to get through.

"The neodim retreated," a young worker said, "talking of releasing gases to immobilize us."

Owen stared at the boy. He looked about nine and had long white hair and ears that stuck out. A wave of compassion swept over Owen, but he had a job to do.

"Hopefully they won't have the chance to use it," Owen said.

When they reached the last workroom, far beneath the other two, Owen gave the order to seal the next room. Using boulders and smaller rocks, the people went to work. Connor looked skeptical as Owen twisted Burden's hairs into a tight strand.

"You said yourself we have no weapons," Connor said. "And we can't leave anyone or the neodim will make them pay. The only alternative is to leave with everyone. And how are you—?"

"If my calculations are correct," Owen said, "we may be deep enough to hit the sealed part of the back of the mountain." He explained what Rachel had told him. Then, dipping the hair into liquid, he ordered workers to place several pitchers full of liquid near the back wall of the cave.

"How do you know how much will make a hole in that wall and how much might bring the ceiling down on us?"

"I don't," Owen said. "But if my chemistry class in the Highlands taught me anything, it is to err on the side of less rather than more."

Howls and cries from the neodim reached them.

"They're coming!" someone cried.

"I hope this works," Burden said.

Owen told everyone to hide in the second chamber and laid the crude hair fuse on the ground. He placed heavy rocks around the pitchers and retreated to the second cave. The young boy with white hair huddled close to the women.

"If I don't make it," Owen said, "take this backpack to my friend Watcher. She'll know what to do with what's inside." With that, he swung the sword on a rock until a spark ignited the wet fuse. It sparked and fizzled, then whooshed into the next room.

"Everybody down!" Owen yelled.

✦

The neodim had assigned two beasts with clinking canisters to enter the small tunnel above the workrooms. They were to open the canisters as soon as they saw the humans, but they had no idea what was inside.

They never had a chance to release the canisters because a bone-jarring explosion rocked the tunnel and quickly filled it with dust. The two finally made it to the workroom, coughing and sputtering. The humans were gone. They checked each of the rooms until they found a new passage at the end of the third. They continued until they came to two jars full of liquid.

"Why would they have left these?" one of the beasts grunted.

A hiss raced up the opening, sparks flew, and a line of fire streaked to the jars. With a flash, the jars exploded, sending a wall of rock and debris on top of them and closing the opening.

51

Back to Yodom

Owen could tell that Burden
was relieved to be out of the
mountain. His steps quickened as they
descended to a cavern with icicles
hanging and a frozen pond. The
ground was snow covered, and the prisoners shivered in their skimpy clothes.

Owen used his sword to heal the
blind, then told them to wait while
he went for help and clothes. But they
did not want to stay, fearing an attack.
Owen sent Burden through hip-deep
snow to find his friends.

After an hour of grumbling (mainly
by Connor), the group was met by a
contingent of villagers Owen didn't
recognize. Watcher popped through,

her face bright. She asked Owen question after question as they headed toward town.

"I have one more job for you when we return," Owen said. He pointed out the young, white-haired boy.

Watcher gasped. "Drushka's son," she said. "Is his father with him?"

Owen pursed his lips. "I don't think his father made it."

Watcher's eyes filled. "What should we do?"

"I'd like to get him back to his mother."

When the group arrived at Yodom, the villagers rejoiced. Owen went straight to the Scribe's house, opened the pouch, and set the metal manuscript on a table.

"This is it," the Scribe said. "And let me guess: you can't read a word of it."

"Exactly," Owen said. "I've tried."

"A precaution by the King," the Scribe said. "He used a special glass to project the words onto the page. I simply copied the letters."

Owen studied the letters, then rummaged around until he found an old windowpane. He put a cloth over one side and held it up to the page. It made a crude mirror, and when he looked at it, he could read the writing.

"Be heartened and glad, for the King's plans will be accomplished. Not one stroke of the pen, not one word of the scroll shall go unfulfilled."

Owen felt his heart would burst, the words filled him with such comfort and joy. His harrowing trip had not been in vain. Toward the end of the first page, he read:

"In the days of the Wormling, the king of the west shall meet with the Dragon concerning an agreement. If he has not already discovered the Son, the Wormling shall travel to the Castle on the Moor and uncover the truth."

"I didn't know there was another king," Owen said.

"Many kings but only one King," the Scribe said.

"And what truth does the writing describe?" Owen said.

"Perhaps to regain *The Book of the King*," the Scribe said. "If the Dragon is there, he may bring it from the other realm."

Owen held his head in his hands. "What about my home? What about breaching the other portals? When will all that happen?"

The Scribe sat and stared at the floor. "I remember once despairing about how much time the writing was taking. I had made several mistakes, and the pages had to be burned and begun again. The King reminded me that our task was not a simple walk by the lake. He said it was more like a row across an ocean. Discouragement would come. Mistakes would be made. But he told me not to be disheartened. He said such were part of the process of calling into being what was not."

"I don't understand."

"Making something out of nothing. Bringing life to a book." He chuckled. "And the King was right. The mistakes actually made it all the more glorious when it was done, because we knew it was perfect."

"And the King knew I would make mistakes?"

"Knew and planned for them. And the next leg of your journey may be the most important, for the king of the west has a daughter who is betrothed to the Son."

"Of course!" Owen said. "Why didn't I think of it? Maybe the Son is already there. Maybe that's where he's hiding, and that's why the Dragon—"

Owen flew toward the door. "I have to find this castle. The Dragon may be going to destroy the Son."

"You'll need this," the Scribe said, handing him the metal scroll. On the back was a map to the Castle on the Moor.

"The King thought of everything," Owen said.

52

Reunion

Connor was planning a siege on the vaxors. Owen could not reason with him and only hoped he would be alive when Owen returned with the Son.

The young, white-haired boy rode Humphrey as Owen and Watcher headed back to Yuhrmer. He seemed glad to escape the mountain and be back in fresh air. Though his hands were gnarled from the workrooms, he giggled like a normal boy.

"Are you going to tell him before we get there?" Watcher whispered.

Owen shook his head. "I don't know how. Could he possibly understand that he has a mother waiting for him?"

The villagers rushed to welcome them, many of the children asking Owen about the dead iskek they had found in the forest. Several of the mothers recognized the boy and hugged him tight, though they had a hard time pulling him from the back of Humphrey; he was having such a fun ride. The boy looked overwhelmed at the attention.

When they brought him to Drushka's home, he sniffed the air and squinted. "I remember this smell," he said. "Bread."

The door opened, and Drushka looked down, hands on hips, as if he were a nuisance. Then a look came over her that Owen would never forget—joy at his return, sadness at the years lost.

Drushka lifted the boy and looked him full in the face, smelled his hair, inspected his hands. She hugged him and spun him, then led him inside. Moments later she rushed back out, dancing and laughing. The boy couldn't stop talking, telling her all that had happened.

Finally letting a friend take the boy by the hand, Drushka approached Owen. "Words can't express . . ."

"Your joy makes it worth everything." Then he whispered, "I have less encouraging news about your husband. I believe he was on his way to find your son but did not survive the climb."

Drushka's eyes left him, and she turned partly away.

Owen put a hand on her shoulder. "His act was selfless and brave. I only wish I could bring him back as well."

Drushka loaded Owen and Watcher with enough bread and cakes to feed an army. Watcher munched on a pastry, and Humphrey couldn't get enough of playing with the children.

Soon it turned dark, and the three were again on their way. As they reached the crest above the town, Owen turned back to look at the stone house. Drushka stood in the doorway, watching her son chase two new friends.

"Why do you stop?" Watcher said.

Owen sighed. "Dreaming, I suppose."

53

The Quest

Traveling at night again, Owen rode Humphrey, ducking limbs, rolling the words of the missing chapter through his mind. It was his lone connection now with *The Book of the King*. His focus had been the section that spoke of the king of the west and the task ahead, but there were other encouraging words.

> A man with faithful friends is blessed beyond measure. It is better to go to battle with friends than with hired soldiers.

Watcher had endless questions about the White Mountain and what

Owen had seen. When Owen described the neodim and the movals, Watcher lowered her ears and asked him to stop. He couldn't help but think she was a little jealous of Burden. Owen had left him in Yodom to help the Scribe and be a sentry. "From blindness to watchman. That is a miracle!" Owen said.

As the days grew colder, it became more difficult to travel at night. Owen could see his breath as they walked, and he shivered against the cold and wetness. During the day they would find a cave or stay hidden in a thicket, sleeping or studying the map.

Watcher sensed invisibles, but they seemed less intense, which concerned Owen. It seemed they should be increasing. Could they have attacked his friends in Yodom? He recalled a passage from *The Book of the King*:

> Continue to travel paths that are straight and turn neither to the left or the right. The King has prepared them for you.

Late one night, Owen was nodding off on Humphrey's back as a cold rain fell. Owen ran a hand through his hair and shook the water out. Lightning flashed, and a low rumble of thunder sounded in the distance.

They had come to a low area with moss hanging from giant trees and muddy bogs surrounding them. Owen heard movement in the water, and as a precaution against attack, he made Watcher walk single file in front of Humphrey.

The farther they traveled, the more difficult it became to find a hiding place during the day. Smelly swamps dotted the countryside. Watcher suggested they just keep going, that there was little demon flyer activity and the trees prevented them from being seen.

But Owen would not be lulled into complacency. "When we least expect it, they can hit us."

Owen thought he heard something wafting over the wet breeze and had Watcher and Humphrey stop. "There it is again," Owen said, pulling Humphrey's reins. "Do you hear it?"

"I hear crickets and frogs," Watcher said. "And rain."

Humphrey shifted under Owen.

"I could have sworn I heard something," Owen said. "Almost like singing."

They walked until first light showed orange and deep blue on the horizon. Just as Owen was about to suggest they find a place to rest for the day, he heard it again.

This time, Watcher stopped and her ears twitched. "It sounds like a lament."

"I thought singing was outlawed," Owen said.

The voice faded, and they continued along a narrowing path, dark water on either side lapping at the edges. From

Owen's judgment of the map, they were less than a day from the Castle on the Moor.

They came to a low, jagged stone wall that ran along the edge of the water. A plaintive sound came over the water.

> *"Sunshine flees; it's cold today,*
> *Cold and wet, they've gone away.*
> *Gone from this world, away from me.*
> *Away, away, away from me."*

The voice sounded familiar, but it wasn't until lightning flashed and he saw the face that Owen gasped.

"Erol," he whispered.

54

A Sad Visitor

Owen slipped down from Humphrey and approached Erol.

"Don't bother coming here," Erol said. He looked sad and weary, eyes red, shoulders sagging. "It will all be over shortly."

"What do you mean?" Owen said, stepping into the bog.

"I wouldn't suggest that. There are gators in these waters. That's what I'm waiting for."

Owen stepped back. "You *want* to be eaten?"

"Not so much that I want to be as that I've lost any reason *not* to be. I've lost everything, Wormling. My only song is a dirge for my children, my wife, and my clan."

Humphrey stomped and fidgeted as Owen stepped closer to Erol. "What happened?"

"The Dragon wiped us out, sent his scythe flyers to open our caves, and then the Dragon himself poured fire down." He closed his eyes and waved a foreleg in front of his face. "My wife tried to protect the children and was cut down."

"Starbuck?" Owen said.

"Fought valiantly but he, too, was consumed."

Owen sat in the dirt by the dark water. Lightning flashed in the distance.

"How did you escape?" Watcher said.

"I have asked that a thousand times," Erol said. "Perhaps the Dragon allowed me to live as my ultimate punishment. To die would have been sweet release. But to be the only survivor, that's the worst—knowing I did not protect my loved ones."

"I'm so sorry," Owen said. "I can't help but think I was somehow to blame. We did hear the news, but I didn't want to believe it."

"It's not your fault, Wormling. Of course, if we hadn't met you and helped you, none of this would have happened, but you must not let it trouble you."

"I would have to be dead for it not to trouble me."

Erol groaned. "Another of your strong traits. You are able to enter into the pain of others."

"I'm coming," Owen said, peering into the darkness of the water.

"You might want to plant your sword and jump."

Owen stuck it in the middle of the shallow bog and swung over to the rock wall. But his sword sank.

"Sword!" he called, but it hissed and bubbled and gurgled under the surface.

"Must be quicksand," Watcher said.

Erol waved. "Probably stuck on the bottom. Wait for morning light and you'll see it."

Humphrey backed away, ears twitching, and Watcher seemed uneasy, but Owen concentrated on Erol. "Come with us. You can avenge your clan's death by helping us find the Son and defeat the Dragon."

"You've been looking all this time. What makes you think you'll ever uncover him?"

Owen pulled out the scroll. "This says there will be a meeting—"

"Wormling!" Watcher said. "Protect the words."

Owen looked back at her, brows furrowed. "We have nothing to fear from our friend. He means us no harm."

"I do not take offense," Erol said. "You have both been through so much. The battle with the iskek and then being trapped inside that mountain . . ."

"Yes," Owen said.

"Did you use the Mucker? Is he still with you?"

Owen took Mucker from his shirt pocket. It was taking the worm longer to recover, but he seemed much healthier than when Owen had left. "Watcher kept him while I . . ." Owen's voice trailed off. He looked up at Erol. "How did you know about the iskek? And the mountain? We didn't tell you about that."

Sudden as a poisonous snake, Erol grabbed Mucker and the scroll and flew off the wall into the water. He quickly became a ravenous crocodile, bigger than Owen had ever seen, and snapped at Owen's leg.

"The Changeling!" Watcher said.

Out of the shadows came cloaked figures that surrounded Watcher and Humphrey, grabbing at them with skeletal hands. Owen couldn't breathe—these beings looked like the same ones who had met with his father!

"Run!" Watcher yelled. She and Humphrey galloped back the way they had come. But the beings subdued them.

"Get out, Wormling!" Watcher yelled.

The crocodile rose, jaws open, teeth glistening.

55

Running

Owen fell back toward the wall as the rocks exploded around the crocodile. In his massive craw was the sword, glistening in the muted light.

"Sword!" Owen yelled and held out his hand, but it stayed inside the croc's mouth.

The Changeling laughed. "You should have listened to your Watcher. She knew something wasn't right."

Owen ran, sloshing through the bog, sinking in mud, then fighting his way out. The croc had disappeared, but now Owen felt the wing flaps of some invisible flyer. He stepped into a deep hole just as a gust of wind whipped his wet hair and a screech passed overhead.

Owen had been frightened of water since he was young, but after the rigorous training from Mordecai, it was his best friend. If he could make it to whatever lay beyond this wetland, he could escape.

Watcher and Humphrey weren't on the path. Owen called for his sword once more but to no avail. When the wings again flapped above him, he ducked and fell into cold water. He swam right, along the edge of the bank, until a splash sent a spray over him.

He dog-paddled to the edge among tree roots and branches and crawled into the tangle, his head just above the surface.

Something moved near him, and Owen brought his legs up, scanning the water. Had the Changeling become the crocodile? a giant python?

Owen climbed branch by branch. Just as his feet left the water, a fish with sharp teeth jumped at him, gnashing and biting.

Piranha! He had seen one in biology class. He'd been there when they fed it steak and watched it tear the meat apart. This was a gigantic one with teeth as big as Owen's hands, and it chewed through the tree roots. Owen tried to kick its head, but as the piranha rose, pulling itself up by biting and lunging through the limbs, Owen jumped down and ran through the swamp.

56

The Panther

The Changeling's brain capacity changed each time he morphed into another being. He shied away from becoming a fish or a bird—never an insect or a tiny animal like a squirrel or a rat. So after munching through the branches as a piranha, it had taken him a while to realize his prey was not in the tree.

He slipped back into the water, closed his eyes, and turned into a black panther. With a shot he was out of the water and shaking it from his fur, his body sleek and muscular. The Changeling ran his tongue over sharp teeth that could tear the flesh of any animal. All he had to do was find this

Wormling, as the Dragon had directed, and bring him to the ground. One twist of his mighty jaws around the puny being's neck and it would be over. Since the Wormling did not have his sword, his friends, or that wretched worm, he was defenseless.

What the Changeling lost in brainpower as a piranha he had gained in ferocity. And now, as a panther, he gained the skill and cunning of a hunter. Nearly impossible to see in this dark terrain, the panther moved with stealth, its eyes sharp, sniffing the scent of the enemy.

With each form he took, the Changeling marveled at the different strengths and weaknesses of animals. While some could speak and reason, others were endowed with great strength or speed. He'd detested being that Erol character, with such a short nose and small body. It had been limiting, for sure, but he did enjoy making music. He tapped into the creature's own musical ability, though he had to make up the sad song, for Erol's family and clansmen had not been killed by the Dragon. The Changeling had merely used the story to exploit the Wormling's concern for others.

Scanning the bog, hugging the ground, the panther sniffed at a few jargid dens and was tempted to run after a deer in the distance, but he stayed on task. He caught a human scent and angled left, snarling, picking each footfall carefully. He came to a knoll in the moor and tensed, sniffing one last time to make sure. Then he sprang over the edge and leaped on the form that lay at the bottom of the dip.

Owen ran, shivering, having shed his cloak in the moor and hoping the Changeling would be thrown off by the scent. He made as little noise as possible slogging over the wet ground, finally reaching the path, where he gained speed. He wished he could somehow soar above the land so he could search for Watcher and Humphrey. He couldn't imagine life without them now.

Behind him a growl and a scream sounded like a 500-pound wildcat. The closest he had been to one of those was watching on television.

Eerie flashes of lightning lit the path. At the next flash, Owen expected the jaws of some huge cat in front of him. Instead he saw the opening to a cave and dashed inside. The back was smooth with a small ledge. He crawled in as far as he could, pulled his legs close, and waited.

His heart still beating wildly, breath coming in gasps, Owen's eyes adjusted. With each flash of light he thought he saw another monster—an iskek, a neodim, a moval.

↟↟↟

Owen Reeder was alone, unless you counted the invisible being next to him—the one looking fondly down at him, the one who witnessed the loss of the missing chapter, the seizing of Watcher and Humphrey, Mucker's kidnapping, and the sword now devoured by the Changeling. The one who had followed Owen this entire time, helpless to intervene until now.

58

Memories

Owen had come to the end of his strength, the end of himself. He had lost the friend who had helped him get to the Lowlands. He had also lost the two best friends he had met, Watcher and Humphrey. He had lost the scroll, *The Book of the King,* and the very thing that gave him confidence in battle—his sword.

In short, he had lost everything.

Crouching in this cave, alone, wet, and shivering, as low as he had been since the death of Bardig, Owen had lost something more: the very desire to continue. Part of him wished that whoever or whatever was chasing him would make a quick end of him.

This despair enveloped Owen as wholly as the cave's darkness. He did not weep; he merely shrank into a tiny ball and sat against the cold stone.

All that was left were Owen's memories.

Memories of friends.

Memories of victory and self-confidence.

Memories of a few words from *The Book of the King*.

> In view of the King's mercy, I strongly advise you to surrender yourselves—mind, heart, soul, and body—as an offering to the one who has called you. By this, you show the King you are willing to serve him fully.

I have surrendered everything, Owen thought. *I did all the King asked, and where has it gotten me? No closer to his Son. No closer to being back in the Highlands. Chased and nearly killed and now utterly alone.*

"But you are closer to the king of the west."

Owen jumped, hitting his head, staring at the darkness. "Who are you? Show yourself."

"As you wish."

Gradually, as sand drips through an hourglass, a man appeared. He looked familiar in strange, shimmering clothing that reached his sandals. He had a short-cropped beard, salt-and-pepper hair, and a pleasant face. But Owen had learned the hard way not to trust a pleasant—even familiar—face.

"Stay where you are," Owen said, feeling for a small rock. "I don't want to hurt you."

The man smiled. "You would if you had to, for you are a fierce warrior, committed to the King. But I have come to help."

Snarls from outside snapped their heads around. A panther prowled at the entrance, its teeth gleaming.

The man raised a hand, and an opening appeared in the cave wall. "Hurry," he said.

Owen had only one choice.

59

Chocolate Darkness

The supernatural exit closed behind him, and Owen found himself in chocolate darkness. He heard the panther through the wall and knew that if he had stayed in that cave, all he would have had to defend himself was the rock in his hand, and he would surely have been eaten.

"Are you here?" Owen said.

"Yes, I'm sorry," the man said, opening his hand to produce a bit of light. The chamber had just enough room for both of them.

"If you're the Changeling, I'll fight you to my death!" Owen said.

The man laughed. "I am not."

Owen wasn't convinced and was

prepared to fire the rock between the man's eyes from point-blank range. "How did you know about this exit?"

"I didn't. I created it for your safety when the panther appeared."

Owen shook his head. "How?"

The man moved toward Owen, hands out, the glow increasing.

Owen raised the stone. "Stay where you are."

The man stopped. "I understand your reserve. The Changeling tricked you, and now your friends have been taken."

How could the man know this if he *wasn't* the Changeling? "Where have they been taken?"

"Moving toward the Castle on the Moor when last I saw them. The Dragon's forces were marshaled to intercept you."

"How do you know all these things?"

"I am Nicodemus, messenger of the King. I have known you for some time. Even in the Highlands."

"Known me?"

"It was my job to follow you, make sure you were safe, ensure you would survive. I knew you were a Wormling before you did."

Owen lowered the rock. "You were the arm in the night that kept me from falling."

"And I was in the school when you were attacked."

"What about here? I've cried out for help a thousand times."

"I was there when you faced Dreadwart, with you on the islands of Mirantha, in the Badlands, and at the White Mountain—"

"I was nearly killed by the iskek. Why didn't you help?"

"Believe me, I wanted to, but I was not allowed. I shudder to think what might have happened had it not been for your Watcher."

"Why would the King not allow you to help?"

"Mine is not to understand but to obey, the same as you." Nicodemus sat and Owen joined him. "Perhaps it was so you could grow, Wormling. Though you have not yet completed your mission, you stood up to the Dragon, injured him. He sees you as the primary threat to his plans."

"He's afraid of *me*?"

"He fears the King and those who follow him. And he fears the Son. You are the key, and he wants you dead. But you aren't, are you? In fact, you are close to reaching your goal."

"How can you say that?" Owen said. "I've lost everything I was given."

Nicodemus leaned close. "The King himself told me to wait until you had lost the book, the missing scroll, Mucker, your sword, and your friends. Only then could I intervene."

"The King knew all this was going to happen?"

"He knows everything. The beginning and the end. Even the Dragon's next move. He sent me to your father long ago."

"What? You spoke with my father?"

"Yes. And he was just as frightened as you when I spoke."

"What did you say to him?"

The being smiled. "I cannot tell you now. But the words were from the King himself. You see, Wormling, it is up to us to follow and obey him. If we do, we can be on only the winning side."

"Are you an angel?"

The man shook his head. "I have powers you might think angelic, but everything I do is subject to the King's approval."

"Where is the Son?" Owen said. "I'm desperate to know."

"Even if I knew, I could not tell you, as the King has forbidden it."

"But the Son is alive?"

Nicodemus cocked his head, as if surprised at the question. "Of course. The King wants you to find him. That is your mission."

"What about my father? my mother? Can you tell me the truth about them?"

Nicodemus frowned. "I regret that I cannot."

"Because you don't know?"

"Because I cannot."

"What good are you if you can't answer my questions?"

"Instead of lamenting what I cannot divulge, focus on what I can."

"Such as?"

"The meeting you discovered between the Dragon and the king of the west will take place. Soon. The Dragon is on his way."

"What else?"

"You must go back to your world, for the darkness encroaches it just as it does here."

"But how can I if I've lost Mucker? And isn't finding the Son my priority?"

"Yes. And discovering him will be next."

"In this world?"

"Yes."

"Is my mother alive?"

Nicodemus stared at the ground, and when he lifted his head, he had a smile. "She is."

Owen's heart leaped. "In this world or the other?"

"That I cannot say. But she is eager to see you."

Owen drank in the news. "And what about my father?"

"Eager to see you as well. But that is all I am at liberty to say. You must not tempt me to go against the King's wishes."

"How do I know you're not just another trick of the enemy to send me off course?"

"Can a house be divided against itself? Would I use the Dragon's trickery to tell you how to defeat him? Courage, Owen. You have been given a great task, greater than you yet imagine."

RHM, the Dragon's trusted aide, met the old beast at their appointed place not far from the Castle on the Moor. The Dragon seemed preoccupied with a spot on his leg. He couldn't stop scratching.

"What news from the Highlands?"

"Quite good, sire," RHM said. "I have personally seen the urchin you spoke of and have confirmed her whereabouts."

"Still imprisoned, as it were?"

"Yes. No one would believe she is royalty. I doubt even her father would recognize her. Is the meeting with him still scheduled?"

"Yes, the preparations have been

made. Have you heard from the Changeling or the raiding party?"

"More good news, sire. The Watcher and the horse have been abducted."

The Dragon sat up. "And the Wormling?"

RHM cleared his throat. "Still being hunted, sire. Our sources believe the Changeling has the sword, the Mucker, and a scroll, but—"

"But not the Wormling?" the Dragon thundered, again scratching at his leg.

"He is defenseless, Great One, without a weapon. With no access to a Watcher, he is susceptible to demon flyers. He has no magic weapon and no instruction from his powerless leader—"

"Who is dead!"

"Yes, you have nothing to fear from this one. If the Changeling does not bring him to you, we will find the Wormling and crush him."

The Dragon looked away, scratching, clearing his throat (which caused black smoke to escape from his lips), and grinning. "If the Changeling does not bring him, we'll crush them both."

When the screams of the panther subsided, Nicodemus disappeared for what seemed like hours, then returned to say they could leave. A door again appeared in the rock, and Owen was amazed at Nicodemus's power.

The sun was up now as the two walked a sandy path between towering trees. Owen feared they might be seen by invisibles, but Nicodemus assured him that he could see what Owen could not.

"Like Watcher," Owen said, missing her and hoping she was all right.

"You could not have had a more trusted companion," Nicodemus said, "though she is prone to loquacious speech."

"You mean she talks a lot? You sure have a big vocabulary."

"The King's is much more extensive than my own, though I noticed as you read *The Book of the King* that he kept it in check. He seems to have chosen words that make his meaning clear."

The sun shone orange on the rippling water. Nicodemus took a long breath. "Do you smell that, Wormling? Water mixed with earth and plants. A sign of good things to come."

"I thought you said the darkness encroaches."

"Shadows must fall before the light invades. You know that from *The Book of the King*."

"It's hard to remember," Owen said. "It seems so long since I held it."

"A fresh wind is blowing; I can feel it." Nicodemus put a hand on Owen's shoulder, and Owen felt warmth flood through him. "You will hold the book again, my friend. And the Son will complete it. And everything written in it will come to pass."

"With all that the Dragon will surely throw against us, how can you be so sure? He wants me dead. He wants the Son dead. And he says the King is already dead."

"He is a liar. The truth is not in him. I believe what the King says, not the way things seem. If we looked only at appearances, you would not have been chosen as the Wormling, would you?"

"Sometimes I wish I hadn't been."

"You would not have been chosen if the King did not believe you would succeed. He would not have given you the power, the book, the sword. Take heart. You will see them all again, along with your friends. While I was gone, I saw Humphrey in a holding pen outside the castle. Watcher was being interrogated."

"You got inside? How?"

"I was given special abilities by the King. Their demon flyers are poor attempts by the Dragon to duplicate what the King did with me."

"Do you have access to the Dragon's realm?" Owen said as they neared the water.

"Yes, but I have been charged with watching you."

"Could you find out where the book is?"

"I could, but again, I have not been given that option. I'm to stay with you."

"But if you're not allowed to protect me, why would you stay?"

"There will come a time when you will need me. I cannot go against the King's orders."

"What good does it do if I find the book and my friends and defeat the Dragon, but the Son is dead?"

"Why think that? I've already told you—"

"I've seen bodies," Owen said. "On the battlefield, through my travels. Many have died."

Nicodemus focused on Owen, his eyes like fire. "Where did you see bodies?"

Nicodemus felt a pang of concern. He trusted the King completely and believed what he had been told, but the King had never actually said the Son was alive. He knelt beside the Wormling, his eyes burrowing deep into the lad's soul. "Tell me about the bodies you saw."

The Wormling told him of many they had buried. "People were also killed in the flood and in the battle with the vaxors. And there was a body at the top of White Mountain—the father of a young man I found inside."

Nicodemus stroked his beard. "Did any stand out to you as possibly the Son?"

"Qwamay was the best candidate, but he turned out to be Mordecai's son."

Nicodemus calmed the boy with his voice. "What do we know about the Son from those passages in *The Book of the King*?"

"He will be filled with virtue. He will vanquish the Dragon, so he must be a warrior. But he will also bring peace, so he is not *just* a warrior. He is a man of the people, because they will honor him. And he was taken and imprisoned."

"What about his stature, his physical makeup?"

"It doesn't say. Perhaps you could sneak into the Dragon's lair and find the book. Maybe I've missed a clue."

Nicodemus shook his head. "We need no more information. We simply need to put together what you have already discovered."

"But I've looked everywhere for him. I've been diligent, followed the King's instructions. I honestly did the best I could."

"I know." Nicodemus sucked in his lower lip, then turned. "It is time I show you something."

He pulled a shining gemstone from beneath his tunic and placed it in the water. An image spread, as if on a liquid crystal display. Nicodemus waved and the display changed. The water blazed orange.

"This is the fire that covered the land after the Dragon

stormed the castle." Again he waved, and the display showed the Castle of the Pines, where the King used to live. "This is the room where the fire began and Mordecai was injured. There—at that exact moment the Dragon blasted him, and there the child is taken."

The Wormling sat as if transfixed.

"The King and Queen became like peasants as they retreated from the Dragon. Here is the burning of the books and the edict by the Dragon that no one should again read or sing."

"Did the King and Queen ever return to the castle?"

"Yes. Sometime later it became safe, though the Dragon kept watch through his invisibles. While the Dragon thought he had the King under surveillance, he was writing *The Book of the King* and making his plans."

When the Wormling saw the Queen crying and running for her life, he wiped his eyes. "Why didn't the King stay and fight? Why did he flee when he has such power and authority?"

"It is not always prudent to use all your force," Nicodemus said. "You must use it at the right moment. The King fled, knowing that if he stayed, his Son might be killed, and with him the hope of a new generation. Through the Son shall all in the Lowlands, the Highlands, and the realm above be blessed, if they remain loyal to His Majesty."

✦✦✦

Owen marveled at the face of the Son. He had brown hair and a mischievous smile, even as a baby. Owen shuddered when beings shrouded in darkness carried him away.

"Where did they imprison him?" Owen asked Nicodemus.

"The vision becomes cloudy at this point. I believe they take him to the Highlands."

"Why didn't the Dragon kill the child?" Owen said. "Wouldn't that have brought the King to his knees?"

"It would have meant the sure destruction of the Dragon," Nicodemus said. "The King would have poured out his wrath on him."

"Which is what the Son will do eventually, right?"

"True. But beings such as the Dragon cannot imagine their own demise. He will do anything for another moment of life, another moment to torture those loyal to the King."

Nicodemus waved, and over the water came the scene of a young girl whisked away by the same dark beings. "This is the princess betrothed to the Son even before her birth."

The father of the girl appeared in anguish.

"That's the king of the west?"

Nicodemus nodded. "Who still lives in the castle and has his own agreement with the Dragon."

"So both the King *and* the king of the west have agree-ments with the Dragon?"

"Correct."

"What sort of agreement?"

The scene shifted, and the Dragon and the king of the west stood over a treaty, the king signing. The Dragon puffed black smoke that clouded the vision.

"Only the two of them know the details. I believe it con-cerns the princess, but we can't be sure."

"What *can* we be sure of?" Owen said.

"That the union of the Son and the princess will culmi-nate the King's plan. And what a union it will be! What a celebration!"

Owen found himself more puzzled than ever, and it must have shown.

"What concerns you now, Wormling?"

"It doesn't make sense. Why did the King allow any of this? If he knew it would happen, he could have stopped it. The Son should be with him right now, without any involvement from me. And who am I?" Owen stood, raising his voice. "Why was *I* chosen? It all seems so random."

Nicodemus spoke kindly, but Owen heard fierce determi-nation. "What *seems* is not what *is*. What *appears* is merely a shadow of what is to come. Trust what the King has put in your heart, Wormling. One day you will understand. Maybe sooner than you realize."

Darkness covered the sun so it shone like blood on the water. Nicodemus looked up, his eyes weary. "The Dragon approaches. I am not permitted to stay with you."

"You're leaving?"

"I will obey, though it may *seem* an inopportune time to go. Those are the King's wishes."

"What am I to do?" Owen said, suddenly feeling the loneliness again. "What of Mucker and my sword?"

Nicodemus gave final instructions and then vanished.

In his place lay a long strand of rope, which Owen picked up. "Why would you leave this?"

A stirring of the water surprised Owen, and he turned around to face the lunge of the most gigantic crocodile he had ever seen.

63
A View from the Interrogation Room

Watcher sat, her legs tied, as RHM questioned her. Worse than his threats was his smell. "If you walk in front of me again," she said, "the contents of my stomach will be on your legs."

"Sensitive, are we?" RHM croaked. "Then tell me what I want to know, and you can enjoy a nice meal of greens."

"I would not tell you the Wormling's whereabouts even if I knew. Which I don't. We were separated early this morning, and I haven't seen him since."

"He's being helped, isn't he? That's what the Changeling said to our scouts."

Watcher gritted her teeth. The

Changeling. They should have killed him when they had the chance.

RHM paced before her, and Watcher felt the bile rising again.

"We now have his sword. We have his precious book of gibberish. We have the missing scroll. We have you and the horse. We even have the tiny worm. Everything but the Wormling himself. Perhaps hearing his beloved friend beg for her life would bring him. Help us, and you won't have to suffer."

"Do what you want with me," Watcher said. "I will never betray him."

"Well, frankly, I've heard that before." RHM moved to a desk and uncovered several glistening steel instruments of torture. He waved a sharp one before her face. "Perhaps you'll change your mind when I—"

The door opened, and a man stepped inside. He was tall with a thin mustache and wavy, brown and gray hair. "I told you I didn't want my home turned into a war zone. Why is this creature here?"

"Are you the owner of this castle?" Watcher said.

"Silence!" RHM said.

"I've done nothing wrong, and—"

"I said silence!" RHM said, raising an instrument of torture.

At the sight of the weapon, Watcher slumped as if lifeless, though she was only faking.

"She is a spy," RHM said. "An accomplice of the Wormling."

Watcher could tell the man was upset. "The Wormling? Here?"

"Just in time for your meeting with His Majesty. The Changeling should have him soon, and if not, I'll use her to lure him."

A chill wind blew through the window, and the man walked toward it. "The sky is darkening."

"His Majesty approaches."

64

Subdued

Getting help from a messenger like Nicodemus is simply not fair. It violates the rules," the Changeling said.

"And what rules are those?" Owen said, struggling with the rope.

"Why, the . . . uh . . . the fair and balanced rules of the land, which I have always abided by in my quests to, ah—"

"Right, by deceiving everyone you come in contact with."

"Well—"

"Quiet," Owen said as he finished hog-tying the croc. "Watcher was right. I should have taken care of you when I had the chance. Where's my sword?"

The Changeling opened his mouth. "It's down here—just reach in and . . ." He opened wide.

Owen shook his head and dragged the Changeling into the cave. He whimpered and pleaded for his life, and when he turned his head, Owen brought a rock down and the Changeling's mouth opened, exposing his gullet. There was no sign of the sword. He was almost ready to dig into the beast's throat when the Changeling stirred.

"You won't find them down there," he said, retching and coughing. "I've already turned your precious things over to my superior. The Dragon has them by now."

Owen grabbed the beast and dragged him toward the rock wall. "Nicodemus, if you're still here, it would be nice if—"

The hole opened in the wall, and Owen threw the Changeling inside. Just as quickly, the wall closed. Owen heard the muffled moaning and whining as he set off again for the castle.

65

The Barn

The Castle on the Moor lay deep
in the middle of swamplike land
even wetter than what Owen had
slogged through. The Dragon's very
presence clouded the entire valley in a
deep fog, even during the day. Sentries
studied the skies as leaves swayed
where no breeze blew. *Demon flyers*.

Everywhere lurked someone from
the Dragon's guard. Owen crept among
the trees, splashing through the water,
espying even more watching eyes. He
couldn't imagine getting to the castle
unnoticed.

But a long ditch angled away from
the castle into the forest, its steep
banks corralling shallow running water

bearing dead leaves and undergrowth. Owen covered himself
with wet leaves and plunged in.

Immediately he was surrounded by fast-slithering snakes with
diamond-shaped heads. Owen had to remind himself that they
were more afraid of him than he was of them, and sure enough,
they moved away as he inched along. When he spotted a guard,
he stopped, hoping his leaf-splattered clothing camouflaged
him. The guard turned, and Owen continued crawling through
the muck, finally making it near the barn. He scrambled up the
steep bank, slipping and wriggling over the edge like a worm,
then crawled on his stomach to the barnyard.

Covered with mud, wet, and cold, Owen desperately
scanned the area for Watcher and Humphrey. Dust and hay
arose near the barn, and Owen pressed himself flat against the
structure. When he was sure no one was watching, he crept
to a creaking door and sneaked in. Nearby guards talked and
laughed or he surely would have been heard.

A whip cracked, and a man stood before the guards at the
back of the barn, hands out to protect the animals. He wore
a floppy hat and a coarse shirt and pants covered with dirt,
manure, and straw. "Please don't hurt them," he squealed.

"Out of the way!" a guard yelled. He flicked his whip, but
the man caught it and pulled, sending the guard flying. The
man was clearly powerful, but just as Owen was about to jump
from his hiding place to help, a second guard attacked the

man with a board to the head. The rest dragged his body to the stall beside Owen.

When the guards returned to the animals, Humphrey stood at the front, back straight, head high.

"Ho, get back there!" the guard yelled, whipping him.

Humphrey reared and took the whiplash under his front, showing his teeth and whinnying. Owen knew he could overpower the guard, but he couldn't take the chance of having him cry out. The guard lashed Humphrey again, and Owen was about to burst.

Another guard joined the first and began separating the work animals from those that would be eaten. From the shrieks of these innocents, Owen could tell what was happening.

Owen rolled into Humphrey's pen, and the horse shielded him from being seen. "Sorry, old friend," Owen whispered. "It's my fault you're here."

Humphrey shuddered flies away and swished his tail in Owen's face.

"Where have they taken Watcher?"

Humphrey dragged a hoof and made an arrow pointing toward the castle.

"What's the best way in? Guards are posted at every entrance, and archers stand at the parapets."

Humphrey looked up and swung his head from side to side.

"Flyers? I should have known." He covered his face. "There's no way in without being seen."

Another animal cried, and Owen peeked between the wooden slats. Wind carried in the fresh, coppery smell of blood. Both guards were covered in red.

"Enough for the feast?" one said.

"We've killed everything from this yard except the caretaker and that horse inside."

"He would be too tough."

"So would the caretaker." And they laughed.

Owen's mind spun, frantic for an idea, one of those wonderful, beautiful ones that would not only get him into the castle but would also bring him face-to-face with his archenemy.

The castle staff, along with the
king of the west and his queen,
stood on either side of the meeting
hall, ready to receive their guests.
Repugnance lined the face of the cook,
a large man with a balding, lumpy
head, but the others stood with faces
cast toward the floor, ready to bow to
the Dragon's every whim.

The queen fanned herself despite
the chilly house. Tiny girls dressed as
maids shivered and rubbed their arms.
Grown men looked like little boys
about to be paddled.

A pack of vaxors sauntered in, waving their swords and axes close to the
workers. The blades were caked with

the blood of some innocent town that had been laid waste. This group made the women recoil, as if they smelled raw sewage.

One vaxor, tall and hairy with red eyes and wearing an animal skin, stuck his chest out like a victorious warrior, but he was not. Daagn had led the failed attack on Yodom and burned to see Watcher suffer. He would make her pay.

As he passed the king, he held his ax at just the right angle to brush the man's cheek. The king recoiled, slapping a hand over the wound. The queen offered a handkerchief.

Daagn sneered, and the king held the handkerchief low, clearly embarrassed. He pushed his wife aside.

Daagn, of course, had not told the Dragon the truth when he had returned from defeat. He had conveyed disdain for troops that had defected or refused to kill innocents. Daagn himself had killed a score of his own. That was his story.

Deep in his heart, where there lay nothing but a desire to kill and destroy, Daagn longed to make up for his failure. He promised himself he would not rest until the Watcher had paid and given up the Wormling.

"All rise for the trusted aide-de-camp," RHM said, "the right hand of the ruler, who goes before the sovereign. Presenting Reginald Handler Mephistopheles!" He proceeded through the line with a wave.

No one so much as looked at him, let alone clapped.

At the end of the procession in front of the vaxors, RHM raised his head and his voice. He recited a long list of accomplishments of the Dragon, battles won, enemies destroyed, and ended, ". . . and soon to be recognized throughout this world and the other as the true king and sovereign over all, the Magnificent One who comes in peace though he could devour all, who comes to speak of treaties signed long ago, ever faithful and wise, all-knowing, His Honor, the Majestic Dragon!"

The vaxors banged their axes on the floor and gave a battle cry as the Dragon, with an impish grin, soaked in the adoration—though it came from only one end of the room. The people at the entrance simply bowed as he passed, some pinching their noses and clearly trying not to gag.

By the time the Dragon reached the end of the line, his tail had just cleared the door. He turned and smiled. "With great pleasure I again visit the esteemed Castle on the Moor. We have business, but now is a time for feasting!"

The vaxors screamed.

"Set the food before me as an offering."

The cook looked right and left, then stepped out. "But we have been held in a room, unable to prepare food."

"I understand the need for security. Come, come, bring the food!"

Two guards in blood-spattered garments dragged the carcasses of the animals they had killed and tossed them on the table behind the king.

"But this has not been cooked!" the cook said.

The Dragon signaled the crowd to move out of the way, took a deep breath, and blew fire over the meat so hot that the table caught fire, along with the draperies and pictures on the wall.

"There," the Dragon said. "Dinner is served."

The vaxors descended like wolves, tearing at the meat and chopping it with their weapons.

67
The Meeting

We are trying to tell this story as Owen would like to read it, stripped of things that might slow the reader. However, the treaty room plays an important role in what is to occur.

In the middle of the large, circular chamber sat a massive, wooden table surrounded by fat, sturdy chairs. Four tall windows ran from floor to ceiling, draped with thick curtains, velvety and heavy. At one end of the room stood a full suit of armor. At the other was an empty bookshelf.

On the walls hung portraits of the king of the west and his queen and a map of the western kingdom. There was also a rendering of the queen with a child in her arms, a girl with a cherubic smile, stubby teeth showing.

The queen took the seat beside her husband, glanced at the painting, and quickly averted her eyes.

RHM and the Dragon stood back from the table, the chairs unable to support the Dragon's girth and RHM not wishing to anger his boss by sitting. Daagn the vaxor pulled out an end chair and sat with his filthy feet on the table.

The Dragon smiled at the king and queen and folded his hands. "Nice of you to open your home. I like what you've done with the place and what has not been done to it, like that other castle we know."

"How is our daughter?" the queen said. "And where is she?"

The Dragon nodded to RHM, who unrolled a scroll on the table, the signature of the king of the west prominent at the bottom. "As stipulated, she remains unharmed, though hidden."

"We have heard rumors of a Wormling," the queen said, brow furrowed.

"Do not be alarmed," the Dragon said. "He is being dealt with and will not be able to reach your daughter."

The king squinted, and the Dragon turned on him. "You wonder why the presence of a Wormling would be bad? He would endanger both your daughter and your estate. This Wormling seeks the Son so that the Son and your daughter might wed. Imagine the chaos. I would have to terminate my agreement with you and, in turn, terminate your daughter."

The queen gasped. "You mustn't."

"Not what I want to do in the least, madam," the Dragon said. "I have your daughter's best interests at heart. However, it is the good of the people that I most care for. The Wormling, if he is not stopped, will make the rabble believe all sorts of nonsense—that they can rule themselves, that they are kings and queens with more power than they can imagine. Such cruel lies give commoners undue hope. Many would needlessly die before they realize how wrong the Wormling is."

"He must be stopped," the queen said.

"All that evil needs to flourish is for good people to do nothing," the Dragon said, his head low. "Do all you can to encourage the people to bring him to me so that I might protect your daughter."

"Yes," the queen said. "Exactly."

The king of the west finally leaned forward. "We have done everything required in the treaty. We have not searched for our daughter. We have not hindered you in any way. We have not contacted the other ruler of the Lowlands. We have met your every demand."

"Yes," the Dragon cooed. "And for that I am grateful."

The king's eyes waxed steely. "But my patience is running thin. Your own treaty states that you will return Onora when the threat to your kingdom has passed." His eyes filled, his lips quivered, and he ran his hands across the table. He looked more like a wounded father than a king.

"Where are my manners?" the king said, dripping with sarcasm. "I should be falling at your feet, begging to wipe the dust off your talons."

A low rumble sounded in the throat of the Dragon.

The king stood. "I should be *thanking* you for taking our daughter, for depriving us of the opportunity to pour our lives into hers, to instill in her our values."

"He's not thinking clearly," the queen said. "Forgive him."

"But then what values do we have left?" the king said. "We who would not even fight for our own flesh and blood. We who would not even stand up to someone who promises us freedom."

"I have given you freedom."

"You have given us slavery! We remain locked here awaiting the release of a baby who in the meantime has become almost a grown woman. We trusted you!"

"This is the first I have seen of your feisty side," the Dragon growled. "For the record, I hate it."

Daagn stood, ax at the ready. "I will cut down the one who dares insult the sovereign!"

The Dragon rolled his eyes. "Be seated." He looked at the king. "And you as well."

But the king leaned over the table, setting both hands atop

it. "Can you possibly understand what it is like to have the thing you care about most in the world taken from you?"

The Dragon spoke soothingly. "I can identify more than you know. You will have your precious daughter back soon. You must realize that I've kept her for her own safety and yours."

The king ran a hand through his gray-flecked hair. "Sure, always for her own good, for our own good. As if we should trust you."

The Dragon rolled onto his feet, a thin line of black smoke escaping his lips. "Your insolence betrays your true feelings. You have pushed me too far." With a snort and a rattle, the Dragon took a breath.

The king moved to a window, clearly unafraid but apparently not wanting his wife harmed when he was incinerated. He opened his arms and with a defiant look said, "Go ahead."

68

Surprise Guest

An old man walked into the room with a live sheep over his shoulders. No one saw the lilt in the man's step or the strength in his arms, which betrayed a much younger man. The Dragon turned and snarled, but the old man kept his head down, seeming to not notice the import of the meeting.

"Matthew," the king said, "the feast is downstairs. Take the animal there."

"Oh, downstairs," the man said. "Silly me." He set the sheep on the floor. It took one look at the Dragon and scurried from the room. The man moved toward a window behind the Dragon.

"Get out or I'll fry you alive!" the Dragon roared.

"Matthew," the king said, "we're in a meeting here. I need you to go downstairs."

The man darted behind the curtains. The Dragon took another deep breath, but before he released it, the man jumped from behind the curtain.

"You wouldn't want to hurt your precious Wormling, would you?"

Daagn shot to his feet, his ax in both hands. "You!"

The Dragon swallowed his fire and covered the vaxor with his tail. "Careful, Daagn. Looks can be deceiving. This is the Changeling I told you about."

"Changeling? It's the Wormling!" He raised his ax, but the Wormling paid him no mind.

"Lower your weapon," the Dragon said.

"But he looks and sounds and even smells just like the Wormling."

"Yes," the Wormling said. "Isn't that the point?" He checked his fingernails and looked about the room. "Much better than that dreary Castle of the Pines. The draperies are a nice touch."

"This is the Wormling?" the queen said, fear in her voice.

"The likeness is startling, eh, Your Queenness?" the Wormling said. "Nothing to be alarmed about. Although I present an exact representation. A clear and convincing voice as well, don't you think, Dr. Flamecough?"

The Dragon had quickly moved from anger to amusement. "He can change into any life-form. Go ahead and show them."

"Yes," Daagn said. "Show us."

"I'm not here for a show. I'm here to report good news."

"Yes?" the Dragon said, sitting up on his haunches.

"The Wormling is dead. Sealed in stone, never to be heard from again, unless you care to slog through that marsh out there."

"Wonderful," the Dragon said. "The Wormling is no more."

"I'm so relieved," the queen said, fanning herself.

"How do we know for sure?" Daagn said.

The Wormling eyed him mischievously and pounced on the table, sitting and swinging his legs. "Always questioning, aren't we, Daagn? Don't you want to move into the shadows around your master?"

"What are you talking about?"

"Oh, that's right. You don't like the shadows as much as you like to run away."

"What's this?" the Dragon said.

"He's making something up," Daagn spat, raising his ax again.

"Am I? You haven't told His Flamethrowingness what happened in Yodom? How you were turned back by rock-throwing children and the Wormling's Watcher?"

"He's lying!"

"Why would I do that?"

"Because you hate me and my kind."

"I don't hate you any more than some disgusting refuse. I just thought your master should know."

"And how do you know this?" the Dragon said.

"I was there," the Wormling said. "I saw the whole thing."

"He *is* the Wormling," Daagn said.

"You admit this is true?" the Dragon said.

Daagn lowered his ax and dropped to one knee. "Indulge me, Your Majesty."

69

Whispered Messages

While Daagn sputtered his lies, Owen moved toward the king of the west. He couldn't simply let the man be incinerated.

Still in character, Owen touched the king's robe and stared into his eyes. "What you said to the Dragon about your daughter—did you mean that?"

Owen could tell the man thought he was the enemy.

"I—I c-came upon the c-camp prepared to wipe them out," Daagn said to the Dragon.

Owen leaned closer, winked, and whispered, "Things are not always as they seem, Your Majesty."

The king's eyes widened. He peeked at the Dragon, then back at Owen.

"I l-lost many men in a landslide ambush they had prepared," Daagn said.

"You call children throwing stones a landslide?" Owen said. He turned back to the king. "Give the vaxors access to your wine cellar. We need them to be—"

The Dragon thundered, "Tell me if what the Changeling said is true, Daagn!"

"My horse is the brown and white spotted one in the barn," Owen whispered. "Ready him quickly."

The king nodded and moved toward the door.

"I did not mean to deceive you, sire," Daagn whined. "If you let me live, I will serve you with—"

Fire shot from the Dragon, engulfing the vaxor. His face melted and he fell, a heap of ash.

The queen moaned and hid her face.

Owen grabbed a pitcher of water and doused the flames. "One down and one to go."

"What do you mean?" the Dragon said.

"The Wormling had something he wanted to say to the Watcher before he was sealed away. The information would be—how shall I say it?—*instructive* to you."

"If the Wormling is dead," RHM said, "we can simply kill her."

"True. If you don't care where that little worm of a Mucker is hiding."

"We have him," RHM continued. "He's back in *The Book of the King.*"

"Perfect," Owen said. "Bring it to me and give me a few minutes alone with this Watcher, and I promise you will be amazed at what you'll discover."

RHM hesitated. "Sire, I don't think—"

"Do it," the Dragon said. "Bring the book."

70

Hard Questions

Watcher, tied to the chair and facing away from the door, snapped awake as it opened. She sniffed the air and craned her neck, though she could not see who it was. Despairing, still she believed that if she died here, the King's plan would carry on. Perhaps with a different Wormling, perhaps with the same—if he had somehow miraculously escaped. He might have to find another Watcher if he had stumbled onto the King's Son and they were making battle plans.

The door closed, and she braced herself for a blow.

Watcher heard a curious turning of pages and strained to turn and see her attacker. Footsteps. A hand gently on her back. "I didn't mean to frighten you."

That was the Wormling's voice! Watcher allowed herself to hope, and a wave of relief swept over her.

He moved into view. "Oh, Watcher, what have they done to you?"

His clothes were grimy and stained, but he held something that took Watcher's breath. "How did you get *The Book of the King?*"

"It's a long story," he said. "Let me unbind you."

Watcher stiffened. "You're not the Wormling! You're the Changeling! You've fooled me twice before but not this time!"

He moved closer and lowered his voice. "Watcher, I swear with my life, it's me. They *think* I'm the Changeling, but Nicodemus helped me subdue him—"

"Nicodemus?"

"I'll tell you later, but we must get out of here."

Watcher narrowed her eyes and looked him over, using all her sensing abilities. Still she couldn't be sure. "Tell me something about you the Changeling would not know."

"I lived in a bookstore with my father. A strange man, a good man named Mr. Page, came in one day and handed me this." He hugged the book to his chest. "The man cut me with a sharp knife."

"But you once told me this Mr. Page was good."

"He was. He took something from underneath my skin. It made me limp."

Watcher leaned forward. "All right. I believe it is you. What is your plan?"

"I've convinced the king of the west to have Humphrey ready."

"The king is not loyal to the Dragon?"

"Hardly. He anguishes over his daughter. I believe his heart still leans toward the true King." Owen tugged at the ropes behind her.

71

Empty

The Dragon sat in a chamber
on the first floor, wincing at
the sound of his vaxors chanting a
drunken homage to his divinity. They
had gotten into the king's wine and
were now reveling and throwing chairs
at each other. The Dragon motioned
RHM close. "Go tell them to shut up
or I'll have them put to death."

When RHM returned, he entered
with the queen. "Sire, the lady wishes
to have a word."

"My dear," the Dragon intoned,
smiling, searching her face.

The woman curtsied. "Begging your
pardon, Your Majesty, but I wanted
to apologize for my husband. He has

JERRY B. JENKINS † CHRIS FABRY

been under such stress. That outburst was unlike him. He knows you will keep your word and that our daughter will be returned safely."

"I came very near to annihilating him. He is a lucky man."

"And I am grateful for your forbearance, Highness."

"I showed great restraint. Had it not been for the Changeling, he would have been hauled out of that room in a bucket, like Daagn. Where is he now?"

The queen gulped. "I'm not sure myself. A servant said he saw him heading toward the barn. He never goes there. I looked out in time to see him bring a spotted horse, not of our stable, to the front of the castle."

"Sire?" RHM said. "That would be the horse of the Wormling. Perhaps the Wormling lives."

"Nonsense. You heard the Changeling."

"But was that truly the Changeling? After you left, we found the clothing of the hired hand behind the curtain. The Changeling never left clothing behind."

The Dragon scratched his chin. "The Changeling entered just in time to stop me from charring the king. . . ."

"And his report sealed the fate of Daagn," RHM said.

"Are you suggesting I erred?"

"Of course not, Wise One. Daagn deceived you and paid the price. I am merely suggesting that the Changeling may not be who he says he is."

The Dragon stood, his face clouded. "Where is he?"

"Locked in the room with the Watcher." RHM leaned closer. "And we have given him *The Book of the King*."

Moving so fast that he knocked the queen to the floor, the Dragon broke through the door and into the hall where the vaxors caroused. They stopped and stared, some diving under tables to escape the flames sure to come.

Instead the Dragon lumbered to the room in which Watcher was locked. A gurgle emanated from his throat, and the guard stumbled out of the way just as the Dragon's stream of fire engulfed the thick, wooden door. Bursting through, the Dragon roared. Watcher's bindings hung to the floor, and the window stood open.

72

Certainty

Owen did not have his sword, but he had the book, Mucker, Watcher, and Humphrey. And that was enough.

However, something troubled him, a memory that kept poking its head out of the ground like a prairie dog. It was of Mr. Page in the bookstore, cutting into Owen's foot.

Quickly, Owen described his meeting with Nicodemus. "Before he left me, he told me this path leads to a rocky area where you can hide," Owen said. "I'll meet you there."

"What?" Watcher said. "You're not going with us?"

"I can't leave the king of the west in danger. The Dragon has to know he helped me."

"And what will you do without your sword? without us?"

"I'll convince the king of the west to come with us and help find the Son, his future son-in-law. And I will retrieve my sword."

"You'll be seized," Watcher said. "I know it. You risked your life for me. I can't let you go back."

Owen shoved the book into his pack and strapped it to her back. "Keep this for me. I can't risk the extra weight."

"I'm scared for you," Watcher whispered.

Owen touched her shoulder. "The words of the book remain the words of the true King. They will be fulfilled, and you and I will enjoy the victory he has promised."

"Together?" she said.

"I am certain of it."

Watcher pulled at the frayed cloak with her teeth until she ripped a foot-long strip. "Look for this material flying high above our hiding place when you return, and you will be able to find us."

73

The King

The vaxors were on the move, stumbling through the courtyard, eyes red and bulging, some heaving onto the ground.

Owen made it to the barn just as a demon flyer's piercing scream sounded overhead. He cloaked himself in a blanket from the caretaker's bedding and peered out the window.

Winged creatures Owen had never seen before descended on the castle. Their wings would span several football fields. The flying monsters carried cages, all but one filled with humans wasted away to nearly nothing. The other bore a new regiment of vaxors in fresh battle array.

The flyers set the cages down near the barnyard and soared away. The vaxors poured out of their cage whooping, frightening the prisoners in the other cages. Owen hoped to dart out and release them, but there were too many vaxors, and the metal locks were enormous.

Suddenly everyone in the castle was driven out—maids, cooks, gardeners, even the caretaker who looked after the livestock. Behind them, pushed like the others, were the king and queen. The king had taken a terrible beating, and his clothes were singed. The queen looked pained.

As the Dragon stalked out, bringing up the rear, RHM hurried along beside him. "End it now, sire. Incinerate them all."

"No, this is the final piece of the puzzle that will accomplish my goal. The people of the land will learn they cannot trifle with me." The Dragon looked to the sky and cried, "Bring me the Wormling and the book!"

A great groundswell of dust arose as invisible beings lifted off.

The Dragon approached the king and queen and smirked. "I could exterminate you now, before your subjects. But I'd rather see you humiliated."

"Please," the queen said, sobbing. "You promised. Our daughter."

"My lady, you will never see her again. Her blood will anoint my throne."

The woman broke down. "I hate you!" she screamed as the king held her.

"If you value your own life," the Dragon said, "you will hold your tongue."

Owen spotted his sword and the missing chapter in the Dragon's talons. The creature mince-stepped, gaining enough speed to get airborne, accompanied by a cadre of flyers in full formation.

The vaxors led the people toward the cages.

A vaxor entered the castle with a torch, and by the time he ran back out, smoke was billowing through windows and doors. The king and queen huddled in their cage, hiding their eyes.

Owen found a dull ax and readied himself. If the vaxors were taken away in their cage first, Owen would break the locks off the other cages before the flying beasts arrived. These people would be a perfect fighting force led by the Son.

Movement behind Owen startled him, and he turned to face another vaxor with a flaming torch.

"So, we have a stowaway, do we?"

74

Caught

Owen sat at the edge of the cage, covered by the caretaker's blanket and jostled by many others pressed in behind him. Enormous wings flapped at the air, making the cage rise and fall like waves on an angry ocean. They were so high that Owen could not see the ground for the clouds. He rubbed the bloody bump on the back of his head.

Someone whispered, "You were fortunate it was a new vaxor who caught you. Velvel would have delivered you to the Dragon."

"No doubt," Owen said.

Others in the cage looked at him strangely. "Who are you talking to?"

The voice again whispered, "I do not want them to see me, Wormling."

"Nicodemus?" Owen said. "You've come to free us?"

"It is forbidden."

Owen closed his eyes, his head throbbing. "How could that be forbidden? I have come all this way, and I'm no closer to my destination than when I first began. Tell me! How could freeing us be forbidden?"

"What do you know of the Son?" Nicodemus said. "That he is courageous. That he will be a great warrior and lead many into battle. That he is shrewd and capable of overcoming the Dragon's schemes."

"Why go over this again?"

"Stay with me. What does *The Book of the King* say about the Son and the Dragon?"

Owen leaned hard against the side of the cage, the wind filling his hair. "That the Son would crush the Dragon's head, but the Son would be wounded."

"Wounded where?"

"In his . . . heel."

"Is there anything you failed to tell me?" Nicodemus said. "Something you failed to recognize about yourself?"

Owen's eyes darted. He was speechless. Finally he managed, "Me? It can't be. I am the Wormling, the one who will *find* the Son."

"But can't a man be more than one thing? A reader as well as a writer? The seeker as well as the sought?"

"No, no," Owen said, writhing. "It can't be. That would mean—"

"What?"

"That the Queen in the Badlands—"

"Is your mother."

It was too much to bear. "And the King is my father." Owen shut his eyes tight, reeling.

And a bride waits for me.

Could it be? Was it possible that all this time, the one Owen had been seeking was himself?

RED ROCK MYSTERIES

BRYCE AND ASHLEY TIMBERLINE are normal 13-year-old twins, except for one thing—they discover action-packed mystery wherever they go. Wanting to get to the bottom of any mystery, these twins find themselves on a nonstop search for truth.

CP0140

The Future Is Clear

Check out the exciting Left Behind: The Kids series